Samuel Smiles Jerdan

Essays and Lyrics

Samuel Smiles Jerdan

Essays and Lyrics

ISBN/EAN: 9783744770552

Printed in Europe, USA, Canada, Australia, Japan

Cover: Foto ©Andreas Hilbeck / pixelio.de

More available books at **www.hansebooks.com**

Yours always
Samuel Smiles Jerdan

ESSAYS AND LYRICS.

BY

SAMUEL SMILES JERDAN.

EDITED BY HIS BROTHER,

CHARLES JERDAN, M.A., LL.B.

" He saw through life and death, through good and ill ;
He saw through his own soul.
The marvel of the everlasting will,
An open scroll,
Before him lay."

TENNYSON.

Edinburgh:
ANDREW ELLIOT, 17 PRINCES STREET.
1878.

EDINBURGH :
PRINTED BY LORIMER AND GILLIES,
31 ST. ANDREW SQUARE.

PREFATORY NOTE.

———◆———

THIS Volume has been prepared in compliance with the request of many friends of the late SAMUEL SMILES JERDAN, who desire to possess his Poems in a collected form.

It would have been printed merely for private circulation, but for the fact that he had so many friends in various parts of the country who may wish to obtain copies, and who are unknown to his representatives.

DENNYLOANHEAD, *1st July, 1878.*

CONTENTS.

BIOGRAPHICAL SKETCH.

ESSAYS.

Shakespeare's Seben Ages.

LYRICS.

Devotional Pieces.

Life Musings.

Songs of the Affections.

Humorous Poems.

BIOGRAPHICAL SKETCH.

BIOGRAPHICAL SKETCH.

―――――◆―――――

" Nature denied him much,
But gave him at his birth what most he valued :
A passionate love　　.　　.　　.　　.　　.
For poetry, the language of the gods,
For all things here, or grand or beautiful,—
A setting sun, a lake among the mountains,
The light of an ingenuous counfenance,
And, what transcends them all, a noble action."

ROGERS.

BIRTH AND PARENTAGE.

SAMUEL SMILES JERDAN was born at Haddington, on the 17th of November, 1846. He
was the second of the three sons of David Jerdan
and Elisabeth Smiles, and was named for his maternal
grandfather, Samuel Smiles, who had been a merchant
in that town. His father, at the time of his birth, was
a bookseller in Dunkeld. His mother was the eldest
sister of Samuel Smiles, LL.D., author of *Self Help*,
Lives of the Engineers, and other popular works.

His mother's mother, in whose house he first saw

the light, was a woman of remarkable intelligence, shrewdness, and force of character,—in fact, a typical Scotchwoman of the last generation. In 1832 she had been suddenly bereaved of her husband, and was left with a family of eleven, the youngest child being only three weeks old. Yet she courageously met and surmounted the difficulties of her situation. Leaving her eldest daughter Elisabeth—who was then only seventeen years of age, but who inherited much of her own ability—to take charge of the children and servants, Mrs. Smiles devoted all her energies to the prosecution of the business on which the support of the family depended. She became known throughout Haddington and the district, not only as a diligent and successful merchant, but as a sagacious and strong-minded woman, who had made up her mind on all the prominent questions of the day, whether political or ecclesiastical, and was ready on every proper occasion to express and defend her opinions. Mrs. Smiles died in 1874, aged eighty-five years, having lived to rejoice in the literary distinction attained by one of her sons, and the general well-being of her family. Dr. Samuel Smiles, in *Thrift*, which was published after his mother's death, refers in a sentence or two to her long and brave life-struggle; and those who read his words, bearing in mind the severe sobriety of statement which is characteristic of all that he writes, will accept this tribute to his mother's memory as at once delicate and touching.*

BOYHOOD.

The parents of SAMUEL SMILES JERDAN removed from Dunkeld to Dalkeith in November, 1847, when their second son was a year old; and Dalkeith henceforth became their settled home. Here the child, who had been very weakly as an infant, quickly developed into a stirring and frolicsome boy. He obtained the first part of his education at a girls' school, where, however, his naturally restless disposition showed itself in innocent boyish pranks to such an extent that it very soon became necessary to place him under the care of a master. He spent his school years, accordingly, first at the Dalkeith Academy, and afterwards at the Dalkeith Grammar School. While at school, he evinced more relish for the society of his playmates than for patient study; although his quick perception and naturally bright intellect enabled him, with far less than the usual amount of application, to make a creditable appearance in his classes. SAMUEL received the ordinary elements of a good English education, and was instructed also to some slight extent in the rudi-

* *Thrift*, by Samuel Smiles, chap. v., pp. 67-8.

ments of Latin and Greek; but his temperament proved too impulsive to allow him to apply himself sufficiently to the study of these languages. He often expressed his regret in after years, when he had come to know the value of classical learning, that he did not make a better use of his early opportunities.

This was all the direct public tuition that he received. He did not enjoy the advantage of "finishing his education" at any first-class academy in the city, much less of attending classes in the University. It will be evident, therefore, to readers of his literary remains, that he must have received by far the larger part of his training after leaving school; and, indeed, that he was in an eminent degree self-educated. The most successful of all curriculums of education is always that to which a man subjects himself; and the brief career of SAMUEL SMILES JERDAN is fitted to remind us that there are strong educational forces in the world besides those that breathe in academic groves, or that are locked up in the classics of ancient Greece and Rome.

YOUTH.

After leaving school, which he did in his fourteenth year, SAMUEL was apprenticed to a firm of wholesale and retail merchants in Dalkeith, and continued in their employment until the autumn of 1866. Here he acquired considerable commercial knowledge, as well as received a careful training in business habits. It was during these precious years of his " teens," too, that the higher faculties of his mind began to awake, and that he showed the first signs of those literary sensibilities and aspirations which were destined to colour to such an extent his brief manhood. The boy became his own schoolmaster. He studied with loving sympathy the book of nature, as it lay open before him on every side, in the classic scenery around "Dalkeith, which all the virtues love." He read daily the book of human character, and became a keen and accurate observer of manners. He began to be charmed with the spell of poetry, growing familiar especially with Longfellow and Tennyson, and poring over the dramas of Shakespeare, till he had made the acquaintance of all the great characters, and could repeat all the noblest passages, in these immortal plays. And he devoured in a desultory way a large quantity of miscellaneous literature, which, however, did not glide over his mind like raindrops over marble, but found receptive soil there, and fell into it as seed.

During one or two of these years he was connected with a young men's literary society in Dalkeith. Although with characteristic waggery he used in after

b

days to recall the humorous side of this experience, and was not slow to mimic certain ludicrous incidents which occurred at meetings when he was present, it cannot be doubted that his membership in this little association supplied him so far with an element of healthful intellectual training.   He took an active part in the debates and essays which formed the usual programme of the meetings of the society.   In the course of his reading he had come to be fascinated with the sad story of Chatterton,—

> " The marvellous boy,
> The sleepless soul that perished in his pride ; "

and, accordingly, one of the essays which he con- tributed treated of the Rowley-Poems, and the won- drous child-genius of their unhappy author.   At the close of one of the winter sessions of the associa- tion, it was arranged that during the summer recess members might engage in a poetical competition on a prescribed subject.   The theme chosen was " The Norman Conquest."   SAMUEL JERDAN was one of four who offered themselves as competitors, the other lads being all several years older than himself.   After reading up the history of the period, and also Lord Lytton's romance *Harold*, he produced a poem, which, although the judges ranked it second in the order of merit, they acknowledged to contain much unripe poetic power, and to be full of promise of future excellence, should its author continue to dally with the muse. His first tale or narrative sketch was called forth in similar circumstances. Its title was "Desperately Wicked;" and a friend who was a fellow-member with him in this juvenile society says of it, that it still dwells in his memory as "a smart clever thing."

All this while, too, SAMUEL was living within the sweep of another influence which he felt to be a perennial inspiration to his mind. The Christian congregation in which he had been brought up, and of which about this period he became a member, was presided over at that time by the Rev. Fergus Ferguson, now of Crosshill, Glasgow. He frequently acknowledged, in the warmest terms, the high privilege he enjoyed in listening every week to the powerful sermons which brought him into contact with an intellect of such incisiveness and brilliancy, and a Christian character so earnest and pure and noble. Not a little that fell from Mr. Ferguson's lips entered into the fibre of his own thought and being, and reappeared by and by in crystallised form in the effusions of his pen.

EARLY MANHOOD.

On leaving his first situation, SAMUEL entered into an engagement as a commercial traveller for a business house in Leith, and gave this migratory life a sufficiently long trial to find it somewhat uncongenial to his disposition and temperament. In 1869 he entered the Excise department of the Civil Service, and was located for a longer or shorter period successively at Edinburgh, Fettercairn, Brechin, and Kirkliston. Having a considerable amount of time at his command, he devoted much of his leisure to general reading, and subjected himself to a course of study in mathematics and philosophy, having read and digested while at Fettercairn Sir William Hamilton's *Metaphysics*, and Victor Cousin's *History of Modern Philosophy*.

It was in April, 1869, that *Bread*, the first of his lyrics written for the *Scotsman* newspaper, appeared in the columns of that journal. The hearty appreciation with which it was received seems suddenly to have awaked within him the consciousness of his latent talent, and unlocked the fountain of his poetic inspiration. He began now to seek in earnest for "the Castalian spring." Although he was at no time a mere mechanical versifier, yet now when any circumstance occurred to stir within him the true poetic impulse, he applied himself with enthusiastic diligence to the cultivation of his muse. So *Bread* was speedily followed in the course of the same season by *Calm and Storm, By and By, Lily, Forsaken,* and other pieces. Most of these, as well as many of his subsequent poems, were copied into other newspapers, both Scottish and English. One or two were contributed originally to the *United Presbyterian Magazine,* others to the *People's Friend,* and others to the *Dublin University Magazine.* Several of his lyrics—as, for example, *Forsaken, The Mermaids,* and *I Love my Love*—were set to music shortly after they appeared, and published in London with considerable success.

In 1872 he was transferred, in accordance with his own request, to the head office of the Inland Revenue, in Waterloo Place, Edinburgh. His desk was in the Stamp department, and he found his new duties there more congenial to his refined and educated tastes than those which he had discharged in connection with the out-door service. His position brought him into daily contact with many intelligent gentlemen connected with the legal profession, and the growing appreciation of his poetical talents made gradual way for him into the society of literary men. He made the acquaintance, among others, of Mr. Alexander

c

Russel, editor of the *Scotsman,* in which newspaper the best of his lyrics continued to appear as they dropped from his pen between the years 1869 and 1876; and he received congratulations upon his literary successes, accompanied with prophecies of greater distinction in the future, from more than one Scottish poet.

Mr. JERDAN began now also to contribute prose papers to various periodicals, in the form of essays, literary criticisms, short tales, and sketches of character. Most of his reviews and critiques appeared latterly in the columns of the *Edinburgh Courant.* His essays and miscellaneous papers were principally written for the *People's Friend. Shakespeare's Seven Ages* appeared in successive numbers of that periodical towards the close of 1874. Among his later contributions was an appreciative essay on " Shakespeare's Songs "—a paper brimful of intelligent enthusiasm for those wondrous lyrics, in which he expatiates on their enchanting grace, their bewitching melody, and their endless variety—as including not only the joyous, sprightly songs of Ariel and Puck, but the dirge in " Cymbeline," and the weird, grating chant of the witches in " Macbeth." In two trenchant articles on " Social Distinctions," he deals out a succession of strong but kindly blows against the hollowness of fashionable life, the meanness of snobbery, and the absurdity of the petty differences which determine the cliques and coteries of modern society.

One of his last contributions to the *People's Friend* was a genial paper on Dr. James Brown's admirable "Life of Thomas Davidson, Poet and Preacher." He had read and studied this book until he almost came to regard the author of *Ariadne* and *The Auld Ash Tree* as a personal friend. Although Davidson and he never met, it is certain that an intense sympathy would have sprung up between them, had they been mutually acquainted. They were both poets. They had similar literary instincts and aspirations. They were both passionately susceptible of the beauties of nature. Both were earnest and reverent students of human character. It could be said of either that he was "a fellow of infinite jest, of most excellent fancy,"—to whom the humorous side of things was seldom long in presenting itself. And yet in both there was the same deep underflow of thoughtful melancholy, which keeps every earnest soul ever musing upon the grave mysteries of life, and

> " Hearing oftentimes
> The still sad music of humanity."

One great charm of Thomas Davidson's memoir consists in the copious extracts from his letters with which the volume is everywhere enriched. The subject of this sketch was of too impulsive and volatile a temperament to occupy much time in private correspondence, and he did not pass through such a protracted course of lingering ill-health as that from which Davidson suffered ; yet there were passages in many of his letters to his most familiar friends which for joyous frolic and delicious humour were not unworthy of being placed side by side with Davidson's.

LAST ILLNESS.

Mr. JERDAN had enjoyed robust health ever since his third year until the close of 1876. About that time, however, his strength began from some unknown cause to decline, and presently it became apparent that a dark arrest had been put upon his eager and active spirit. In the spring of 1877 the first symptoms appeared of the insidious disease that was to cut him off nearly a year afterwards. For several months the highest medical skill was baffled in endeavouring to determine the nature of his ailment. But it was already too painfully evident to his friends that there was no longer the old light on his face, or the familiar buoyancy of spirit which had always belonged to him.

At length, in the end of July, it was discovered that

he was suffering from one of the forms of the terrible malady known as Bright's disease. The symptoms were intermittent indeed, and this was the reason why a diagnosis of his case had not been accomplished earlier; yet there was little reasonable prospect that the remainder of his life would be anything better than that of an incurable invalid,—marked out for an early death. So long as there was even a slender hope of recovery left to him, he clung to it with all the tenacity of his intense nature ; but, as soon as he became convinced that Providence had willed it otherwise, he resigned himself to his lot, and began to " set his house in order." He remarked to a friend one day, after reaching this conviction, that *he felt now as if some one had tapped him on the shoulder, and told him that he was wanted elsewhere.* From the beginning of winter he was constantly confined to bed. His sufferings were continuous rather than acutely severe, and he bore up against them with much manly fortitude, maintaining a cheerful spirit throughout his long weary illness, and often lighting up his sick-room with gleams of the old strongly-flavoured wit and gentle humour. Until near the end he found it difficult, in the presence of those visitors in whose society he delighted, to reduce his spirits to a degree of tranquillity befitting his physical weakness ; for he often wore himself out in entertaining them with his easy flow of intellectual conversation, intermingled with sallies of merriment, and sent them away wondering if he could be so very seriously ill after all.

His long illness, distressing though it was both to himself and the family circle, proved a great blessing to him. He had for a considerable time been thoughtful and earnest in relation to the most important of all matters, as the general tone of his lyrics abundantly reveals; but the growth of his piety during the last months of his life was unmistakable. He remarked sometimes that although he was not accustomed to speak much as to his spiritual experience, this was not because he did not think much and deeply on spiritual things. During the earlier stages of his illness he was occasionally troubled with doubts and difficulties as to various practical questions connected with theology; but before the end drew near the sky of his faith became clear of every cloud, and he was able to rest with a simple, peaceful trust upon the righteousness and love of the Redeemer of men. His own experience during the last weeks of his life was most accurately reflected by anticipation in his own lines written years before :—

> " The eyes grow dim. O LORD of Light !
> To Thee are stretched hands pale and thin :

> The shadows, deepening with the night,
>   Still gather in.

> " Darker—more dark ; a night there is
>   On which the morning ne'er shall break ;
>   But we have hope—our plea is this :
>   ' For JESUS' sake ! '"

During the last three or four weeks his frame was sadly wasted ; and more than once he was not expected to survive longer than a few hours. But the light flickered up again and again before it was finally extinguished. At last, on the morning of Tuesday, the 26th of February, he passed gently away.

He enjoyed during his long illness the loving companionship of one whose presence more than that of any other could minister solace and comfort to his spirit. Her devotion all through the various stages of his dark experience was very beautiful. She was never long absent from his sick-chamber until the last scene was over, when

> " That remorseless iron hour
>   Made cypress of her orange-flower."

His own lyric, *The Night-Lamp*, though it was written four years before his death, and when he was in the full flush of manly vigour, seems almost prophetic of the loving and tender ministry which was to prove such a blessing to him during his last illness.

He was buried in one of the old graveyards of Dalkeith beside his mother, who had gone before him in 1871, and whose removal had drawn from him a touching little poem *In Memoriam.* The only intimation of his funeral was a general one, given in the newspapers; yet there was a large spontaneous attendance, many private and literary friends having travelled a long distance to be present. His coffin was strewn with wreaths of white flowers—a silent, subdued expression of " the blessed hope " which made his end so calm and peaceful. " He asked life of Thee, and Thou gavest it him, even length of days for ever and ever."

The Edinburgh newspapers, when his death became known, expressed in graceful language their warm appreciation of his talents, and their regret that such a bright and promising career had been so prematurely brought to a close. Nor did he lack the tribute of poetic sorrow; several monodies to his memory—some of them of great merit—having appeared in various periodicals.

> " He knew
> Himself to sing, and build the lofty rhyme ; "—

so his friends felt that, when he passed away, they must sing for him, and accord him " the meed of some melodious tear." We cannot deny ourselves the pleasure of quoting one of the sweetest of these funeral poems—that of his friend, Mr. L. J. Nicolson :—

"IN MEMORIAM :

"SAMUEL SMILES JERDAN.

"We met, and walked a little space, and now
    I see thee lying in thy lowly rest,—
Pale silent lips, closed eyes, and darkened brow :
    And I am dumb, for surely God knows best.

"The flowers are coming forth to welcome spring,
    The singing time of birds is now at hand :
A tender memory to us they bring,
    For thou art gone into the Silent Land.

"And we shall miss thy voice along the way ;
    So much less music on our ears will fall ;
The great world rushes on from day to day :
    One singing heart is silent—that is all.

"The song is hushed that was so well begun,
    To add a name to unfulfilled renown ;
And now we come with tears, when day is done,
    To leave on thy dead brow the poet's crown."

PERSONAL APPEARANCE AND CHARACTER.

In stature SAMUEL SMILES JERDAN was tall, although, during the last years of his life a slight stoop made him appear somewhat less so than he really was. His personal appearance and bearing were prepossessing.   He inherited the likeness of his mother. His complexion was fair and ruddy, his features good, and the expression of his countenance pleasing. The photograph prefixed to this volume was executed about four years previous to his death, when he was twenty-seven years of age, and is an excellent likeness.

It would be difficult for the writer of this sketch to speak at length about his character.   But the less need be said here, seeing that its prominent features are exhibited to a large degree in the simple enumeration of his literary remains.   Those who read between the lines of this volume may not only discern for themselves the thoughts of his heart, but contrive also in some measure to limn the expression of his mind.   He was not accustomed to speak much of his deepest sympathies; but they come out abundantly in his poems.

His intellect was acute and nimble rather than strong, and brilliant rather than profound.   He was fond of an occasional brisk intellectual discussion, and was not slow to detect any flaw in the reasoning of his opponent.   He excelled in repartee.   He had great facility as a mimic.   His power of sarcasm was somewhat formidable; but, although a little warm-tempered when unduly interfered with, he did not allow himself to indulge in any raillery severe enough to cause injury to another's feelings. He was naturally of a restless and impulsive disposition; but the impulses to which he yielded came from a warm heart and a generous mind.

Shy and reserved in manner towards strangers, he was uniformly sunny and buoyant in the presence of intimate friends. Although always chary of speech in large companies, he seldom failed to brighten up each little circle of familiar acquaintances with his irrepressible wit, and his constant flow of kindly humour. His keen sense of the ludicrous, together with his literary accomplishments, and the sprightliness and versatility of his nature, gave a charm to his companionship.

These qualities were united with a quick sense of honour — a supreme contempt for all shams and shabbinesses—an admiration of every action displaying genuine principle or common-sense, and a kindly, loving interest in humanity at large. He had little patience, indeed, with any person who appeared to be "wise in his own conceit." A friend has truly remarked that one striking feature of his character was "the *sang froid* with which he cut through the little pomp and dignified airs of some men." Yet no one appreciated more than he all that is attractive and beautiful in human nature. His love for his own kindred and friends was deep and subtle. He had an intense sympathy with the struggles and sufferings of the poor; and this chord of his nature vibrates again and again in his lyrics.

He rejoiced in all things that are lovely and of good report, and delighted to read and study only what is pure. He had no sympathy with what is called "the fleshly school" of poetry. In his own writings he "uttered nothing base"—

> "Not one immoral, one corrupted thought,
> One line which, dying, he could wish to blot."

LITERARY REMAINS.

As already remarked, Mr. JERDAN's prose writings took the ephemeral form of popular magazine articles and newspaper reviews. His literary judgments as a reviewer were acute and catholic, and they were usually expressed in language at once terse and graceful. The *Scotsman* newspaper, in noticing his decease, remarked that his prose contributions "justified the belief of his friends that, if his life had been prolonged, he would have attained a not undistinguished place in English literature." He did not, however, take all the pains which he might have done to perfect his prose style; and this is to be

traced partly to his impatient temperament, which ·
would not allow his mind to linger very long over
any matter, and partly to the humble estimation in
which he always held his own literary abilities.
While his periods, therefore, are always expressive,
and often elegant, they are occasionally wanting in
sustained energy and rhetorical fulness.   Still, despite
this defect, his prose always attracted from its tenderness of humour, added to those elements of colloquial
grace and ease which marked it to be the natural
outflow of an accomplished and versatile mind.

The series of papers on *Shakespeare's Seven Ages* is
included in this volume, as being, upon the whole, the
best available selection from his essays.   Should these
papers appear somewhat slight in form, and repetitious
in statement, the reader will kindly notice that such
qualities are due to the circumstance that the series
was given to the public anonymously in successive
numbers of a weekly popular serial.   It is believed
that their presence in this volume, so far from impair-
ing its unity, may even be advantageous as a not
unsuitable introduction to the poems which follow.
For Mr. JERDAN's friends discerned running through
the *Seven Ages* not a little of that delicacy of thought,
fertility of imagination, and felicity of language, which
characterise his lyrics.   This group of essays reflects

the author's poetic instincts, and is itself, in fact, at least in some degree, a prose poem.

Mr. JERDAN's essays and critiques were valuable chiefly because of their promise; but in his poetry, now for the first time collected, there was not only still larger promise, but also a measure of solid and enduring performance. His muse was essentially lyrical. His poems are almost entirely subjective : they express his own individual thoughts and emotions, and view the outer world chiefly as reflected in the experience of his own life. Only twice did he attempt the popular ballad, or minor epic, though not without success, in his *Maid of Norway*, and in *The Galloway Wife.* And his only dramatic experiment is his *Fragment from Goethe.* It accorded with his nature, too, that his poems are all brief, and that he did not assiduously gird himself, as others with his gift might have done, to any more serious and prolonged endeavour.

His lyrics embrace a great variety of theme. The editor has ventured to classify them roughly into four groups. Of the " Devotional Pieces,"—all of which show the depth and fulness of his religious feeling,— four are new-year hymns, written by request, for use in a Sabbath school, of which his younger brother was superintendent. The themes of the second group, entitled " Life Musings," were almost all self-suggested ;

and this group contains some of his finest productions. The third group,—" Songs of the Affections,"—finds its centre in the balmy, bracing associations of family life, and in the sweet despotism of the gentle passion. And in the fourth group,—the " Humorous Poems," with which the volume concludes,—a fresh, rich vein of poetic faculty begins to be opened up, but only so far as to induce regret that he was not spared to work it more fully.

Some of his poems contain descriptive passages, as *The Owl, The Meeting, Inchkeith, Telegraph Wires, Windygowl.* One at least—*The Song of the Reds*— throbs in its every line and syllable with a pulse of fire. His muse, however, very rarely indulged in vehement passion. Usually his verses give the impression of a heart looking with pensive eye upon the sorrowful side of life, and his prevailing strain is that of melancholy tenderness. There is true pathos in such pieces as *Alone, Back to the Hamlet, Steer Straight for Me, Unbaptised.* Some little incident which came under his own observation, or which struck him in the course of his reading, and which another mind might not have observed at all, he would revolve awhile in his fertile fancy, and presently issue enshrined in a clear-cut, suggestive, " solemn-thoughted idyll."

And his poems claim attention for their execution

no less than for their conception. Although of unequal merit in this respect, they combine to show decided skill in the treatment of incident, and considerable taste and cunning in versification. He constantly varies his metre, and yet each measure seems always quite pliable to every emotion which he desires to express. His verse is generally clear as a running brook, and as full of liquid melody. He has not left many weak lines, or lines where the words seem yoked together awkwardly and uncomfortably. His rhymes are almost always true. And, taking it all in all, it has been admitted that his lyrics wed thought and expression with sweet becomingness, and that his touch is one of bright finish and delicate beauty.

In these remarks the writer has not been merely giving expression to his own judgments. He has been trying to gather up the opinions of that select circle who were best acquainted with his brother's literary merits, and of those genial critics connected with the press who have written appreciatingly of the place which SAMUEL SMILES JERDAN had begun to occupy in the guild of literature. It was conceded by all who knew his writings, even in the forms in which they originally appeared, that he had been a free-born citizen in the commonwealth of letters. And the purpose of this sketch and volume has simply been to lay a modest *immortelle* upon his grave.

Thomas Davidson and he were both thirty-one years of age when they died ; and a short sentence which he wrote about Davidson may now be applied to himself :—" Whom the gods love die young ; and he, like many other poets, lived only long enough to enable us to ask, ' If this was his youth, what would his manhood have been ? '"

C. J.

ESSAYS.

ESSAYS.

◆

𝖘𝖍𝖆𝖐𝖊𝖘𝖕𝖊𝖆𝖗𝖊'𝖘 𝖘𝖊𝖛𝖊𝖓 𝖆𝖌𝖊𝖘.

FIRST.—THE INFANT.

"All the world's a stage,
And all the men and women merely players :
They have their exits and their entrances ;
And one man in his time plays many parts,
His acts being seven ages.   At first the Infant,
Mewling and puking in the nurse's arms."

THE two best books in the world, it has been said, are the Bible and Shakespeare.   Hundreds and thousands of other books have been written about these.   Who could number the dissertations, essays, criticisms, commentaries, lectures, sermons, refutations, acceptations, which have been written about the Bible?   In more senses than one it might be called "The Book of Books."   Shakespeare's text has also undergone an amount of analytical and

B

critical examination second only to that of Holy
Writ; while whole libraries have been written about
the life, religion, and philosophy of the poet. Certainly fewer lectures or sermons have been taken from
Shakespeare than from the Bible, and it is right that
this should be the case; but in the present instance
we mean to found our remarks upon a single clause
from the poet's works. We are not going to be
exegetical; we will not make vague guesses about
his life, of which so little is really known; but we
propose to take a short text from the works of the
great dramatist, and see what can be drawn from it.
Although we take a text, we do not intend to preach
a sermon; we shall perhaps moralise and philo-
sophise a little, as the humour suits us, and we shall
be grave or gay as the occasion requires—but we
hope we shall be oftener gay than grave.

Before raising the curtain upon the first Act of the
play, let us pause for a moment and think of the
strange theatre in which we are. If all the world's
a stage, where is the auditorium? Before whom is the
life-drama played? The wide universe must be our
theatre. There are spirits around us "both when we
wake and when we sleep." They heard the morning
stars sing the prelude at creation, and they will
witness the great *denouement*, " The one far-off divine

event to which the whole creation moves." We as actors cannot well be impartial spectators of what is going on around us. We have each our little part to play, and the whole history of time would be incomplete without the quota contributed by the most insignificant of us. Each individual life may, as it were, be a complete thing in itself; but it is also a contribution, and a necessary one, to the full history of humanity. A nation has quite as distinct a life as an individual—it is born, grows old, and dies; and as a nation is only a number of individuals, so the world is only the aggregate of nations, and has its history, which is now being wrought out.

Surely the highest study to which man could direct his attention is this Philosophy of History, or, as Herbert Spencer has termed it, this Science of Sociology. There is a great play, drama, tragedy, or whatever it might be called, gradually unfolding itself with the years and centuries; and had we but eyes to see, could we read the signs of the times, we might become wiser than prophet or seer. But it is not with the history of the world we have to do, so much as with the history of a life. Shakespeare's Seven Ages are the development of the individual. Truly each man in his time plays many parts. Ah, how inexpressibly sad and tragic have not many lives been, and what a sermon might be preached simply from the text, "There lived a man !"

We said, however, that although we had taken a text, we were not going to preach a sermon. We rather fear the gentle reader will think we are breaking our promise by writing in this serious vein. Perhaps some of our lady readers—matrons and maids—from the title of the paper expected a few hints in regard to the management and training of little ones.

"What about the baby ?"—is the question we imagine being put to us; and certainly it is quite pertinent, and we must produce him at once, instead of wondering what is to be the ultimate destiny of the whole creation. Perhaps the reader has heard of the German philosopher who never saw a camel, but evolved one out of his own consciousness. Well, we cannot say we have never seen a baby, but as it is necessary now that we present one, we doubt we must follow the example of the philosopher. Our text demands it ; so—*ting-a-ling*—up goes the curtain —there it is—BLESS IT !—

."Mewling and puking in the nurse's arms."

Did we say IT ? Pardon us, kind ladies ; we should have said HIM. We have offended in this way before, and been rebuked, our fault being the result of ignorance and inexperience, boy and girl babies looking so much alike to our eyes, that we did not wish to commit ourselves as to which was which. In this case, however, we know that *it* is a boy. So we must correct ourselves and say, " There *he* is—bless *him !* —red, very red—blushing for all the follies he is about to commit" (as Bulwer Lytton has said). Let us have a look at him, with his scarcely perceptible nose ! He is creased and crumpled as an undeveloped poppy-head, and about the same colour as a full-blown one. Watch him waving about his little doubled-up fist, as if he were trying to comprehend space, and meant to fight boldly in the life-battle. Listen to the feeble cry !—that voice will become a stentorian bass by-and-by, and the little tiny arms will be strong as iron bands.

This is a man born into the world ;—and how much is expressed in that statement ! Another immortal soul brought into being—something infinitely greater than the great round world itself ! Another creation in Time ! Has this soul waited on the tedious shores of Lethe until now ? What is its mission here—its destiny—the object to be served by its life ? It comes from darkness, passes for a moment through the sunlight of this world, and then again fades from human sight.

Many a mother, while looking at her child, has mused in this way; and, straining eyes far into the future, has wondered, "What will this little one become?" The possibilities that are in him nobody can tell, and time itself alone will show what use he will make of these possibilities. This babe may perhaps, after all, be one of the world's great ones. Alexander would look wonderfully like this child at his age, and doubtless when Homer was young his song would be no sweeter.

We must not anticipate, however, or build any castles in the air; our infant is an infant pure and simple, and his part of the play is just to be as complete a child as possible. He must be weak and tender: the tenderest babe, it has been said, often becomes the strongest man.

Is it not strange that man, who is the greatest of all creatures, should also be the weakest of all creatures when young? A baby requires far more gentle and tender nursing, and that for a much longer time, than the young of other animals. This is surely an indication of the faith the Creator has in the tender loving delicacy of woman, and of her ability to help the helpless and nurse the weak. A most cursory glance at the young of other creatures will establish the fact of the extraordinary helplessness of man. A chicken can pick for itself, although the shell from which it emerged be yet sticking to its back.

Rousseau, in his *Emilius,* says that the chief art in an infant's education is to *lose time.* Mothers are apt to wonder at the rapid progress their children make, and talk about it; in our estimation the cause for surprise rather is the exceedingly slow advances made in physical strength and mental power by children.

Mansie Wauch was astonished, at Benjie's birth, when he discovered that he *saw,* and was not born blind, like a puppy. Although children are born with sight, however, everybody knows that it is a long time before they can distinguish objects; at first they see everything in general, and nothing in particular. The same thing may be said of any of the other senses. The nurse's lullaby, at first, is sung to an ear that hears it not; for a long time the child cannot distinguish sounds. A baby's little hands are so feeble that he cannot even arrange his fingers at first to grasp anything. Think of the time which elapses before a child can walk or talk. At birth the mind is as feeble as the body—it is a *tabula rasa,* as it were; and knowledge comes by experience, and after the power to know has, by exercise, been acquired. The brain is in a sort of jelly state in the infant, and it requires to become firm before it is of much use for thinking. A young lamb or foal will know its mother by sight in two days; it is a very long time before a young child can tell its mother from anybody else. Lord Dundreary says he laboured under the hallucination for six months that a glass bottle with an india-rubber stopper was his mamma.

The baby proper only performs the offices which Shakespeare has attributed to him in our text; he crows and kicks, throws about his little limbs, twists and writhes,—gathering strength in every muscle for the battle which is to come. He knows nothing of himself, or of you. He sees men as trees walking; but by-and-by the film will pass from his eyes. The five gateways of knowledge, the senses, will soon fill the little head with the experiences of us all; he must just bide his time. Nobody knows when the first glimmerings of self-consciousness take place. Tennyson has beautifully expressed it—

> " The baby new to earth and sky,
>   What time his gentle hand is prest
>   Against the circle of his breast,
> Has never thought that ' this is I.'

> " But as he grows he gathers much,
>   And learns the use of ' I ' and ' me,'
>   And finds ' I am not what I see,
> And other than the things I touch.'

" So rounds he to a separate mind,
From whence clear memory may begin,
As through the frame that binds him in
His isolation grows defined."

And when his isolation grows upon him the season of infancy is past. The baby is born newly into the world—to him everything is new. He has eyes and hands, "organs, dimensions, senses, affections, passions." He is an heir of the common lot, and will be a sharer in the joys and sorrows of our common humanity.

It will not do, however, to keep the curtain up too long upon our babe. We have shown him as he is, and, like all parents, we think him a wonderful *wean*. He is weak and feeble, but he will kick himself into strength. As we let the act-drop fall upon the first Act we will wish " more power to him," and when the curtain again rises it will be on a child of a larger growth.

SECOND.—THE SCHOOL-BOY.

" And then the whining School-boy, with his satchel
  And shining morning face, creeping like snail
  Unwillingly to school. "

IN our last paper we discussed the first of the Seven
Ages—" The Infant, mewling and puking in the
nurse's arms." We introduced a little red baby to
our readers; we handled the subject gently, dandled
it as it were, and as was fit. We examined the
youngster physically, and moralised about him in all
his tripartite nature. We showed that he was in a
very undeveloped state; but we remarked that, in
the ordinary course of time, he would emerge from
that dim chrysalis condition, and grow strong in
body and in mind.

When he entered the world our baby was, to use
an apt expression often applied to infants, "a little
stranger;" nobody had ever seen him before, and he
had never seen anybody before. The whole material
world required to be introduced to him, while even
with his own senses, through which that introduction
alone could be performed, he had the very slightest

acquaintance. We said, quoting Rousseau, that all the infant had to do was to lose time. He must wait days, weeks, months, years. Simply give him food for the body, and let the mind take care of itself, and time will work wonders. He will *look*, mark, and inwardly digest.

Our baby has done all this; and as he is intended to be a fair average specimen of the race, we may just indicate in a sentence a little of the progress he has made. He was a stranger at first, and made ugly faces at his best friends; a little time cured that; he drowned a hundred sorrows at the maternal breast, and looked up one day, *seeing* and *knowing* to a certain extent. Some months passed; the little one could creep about on the floor, and laugh, and kick, and captivate all hearts by his winning ways. One day his mother sets him down alone, holding by his little chair; she goes three steps back, stoops down, and says, "Come, steady, my boy!" One or two tottering steps, and he falls into the outstretched arms, and is fondled and kissed, and tossed in the air, and gloried over; for a mother's heart is the same since the world began.

This is perhaps the most interesting period in the growth of a young child. Then there is the first attempt at producing an articulate sound. Speech has small beginnings, like every other gift. The first faint smile that plays upon the features of a babe is an indication of the infinite superiority of the child to the young of any other creature. Man is the only animal that laughs. But if the first smile shows the superiority of the child, the first word, distinctly pronounced and understood, is a crowning indication. Well, Time has taught our infant to walk and talk.

We promised in our last paper that in our next we would consider a child of larger growth. We must suppose that years have come and gone—the seventh part of a life has passed away. The child has learned much—we cannot pause to consider how much; but we shall raise the curtain on the second Act of our play, and show him on his way to learn more; and in doing so we quote our text :—

> "Then the whining School-boy, with his satchel
> And shining morning face, creeping like snail
> Unwillingly to school."

It is observable in this piece from Shakespeare— "The Seven Ages"—how very apt, appropriate, and terse are the few words given as the description of each Age. No other words could be found which would be as true or applicable. It is a kind of telegraphic writing—condensed, pithy, boiled down. We have the whole history of a life in a few lines, and each line is so suggestive that a book might be written about it.

Each line is only a hint, a touch, an outline, the reader himself being allowed to fill in the details. We have this description of the School-boy as an instance.

We can imagine we see him on the road to school, and there has been much preparation to get him there. His mother, or nurse, has dressed him and scrubbed him—polished his face with soap and towel until his cheeks glisten like ripe tomatoes. We remember we had a nurse who polished up our face in the same way. She was a strong woman, and used a rough towel, and rubbed up and down our face as if it were a flat surface, where there was no nose. Well, the boy has been dressed, and breakfasted (on porridge, we hope), and, with satchel on his back, his mother gently pushes him out, and off he must go, however unwillingly, to school.

And he does go unwillingly—why? It is a glorious summer morning; the lark sings sweetly in the sky; the little burn by the roadside chatters and ripples over its stones, glittering in the sun,

> " With here a blossom sailing,
> And here and there a lusty trout,
>   And here and there a grayling ;"

a rabbit darts about in the field there ; butterflies dance in the sun ; all is bright, and fair, and free. But the boy must not linger too long by the way to enjoy it ; yonder is the village school, where he must remain cribbed, cabined, and confined; and, should he be too late in arriving there, the pedagogue will "whip the offending Adam out of him." Goldsmith describes the teacher well, and we hope to be pardoned for quoting his graphic lines :—

" Beside yon straggling fence that skirts the way,
   With blossom'd furze unprofitably gay,
   There in his noisy mansion, skill'd to rule,
   The village master taught his little school.
   A man severe he was, and stern to view ;
   I knew him well, and every truant knew.
   Well had the boding tremblers learn'd to trace
   The day's disasters in his morning face ;
   Full well they laugh'd with counterfeited glee
   At all his jokes, for many a joke had he ;
   Full well the busy whisper, circling round,
   Convey'd the dismal tidings when he frown'd.
   Yet he was kind, or, if severe in aught,
   The love he bore to learning was in fault.
   The village all declared how much he knew—
   'Twas certain he could write and cypher too ;
   Lands he could measure, terms and tides presage,
   And e'en the story ran that he could gauge.
   In arguing, too, the parson own'd his skill,—
   For, e'en though vanquish'd, he could argue still ;
   While words of learned length and thund'ring sound
   Amazed the gazing rustics ranged around—
   And still they gazed, and still the wonder grew
   That one small head could carry all he knew."

This, then, is the schoolmaster who is to teach our

boy the three R's. We can sympathise with the slow pace at which he moves along, being aware how little the youngster knows of the necessity of school attendance. But it is a necessity; he must learn to read of heroes, and by-and-by he will emulate their actions even at " the cannon's mouth;" he must learn to write, that by-and-by he may pen a sonnet " to his mistress' eyebrow." A portion of the immense knowledge stored in the head of his instructor will be imparted to him, and by-and-by he will recall a little of it in his " wise saws and modern instances."

Shakespeare says—" All the world's a stage," and it might with equal truth be remarked that all the world's *a school.* Man is learning all his life. We have shown what the infant learns: he is detained at home until he has learned enough to fit him for school; he is detained at school until he has learned enough to fit him for the teaching of the world. The little village school is itself a miniature world. The teacher is its autocrat—he makes its laws, and punishes and rewards as these laws are kept or broken. There the boy mingles with his fellows; he competes with them, he finds his level among them, out-distances some — is perhaps out-distanced by others. At school he has exactly the same struggle and fight, and the same difficulties to struggle and fight with, as he will have in the larger world outside. There is no royal road to learning; and in the little school, as in the big world, *brains tell.* We must, however, qualify this remark by saying that, although brains do much, the power of steady application may perhaps do more. Remember the fable of " The Tortoise and the Hare."

So much, then, for the difficulties and earnestness of school-life. Let us now speak of its enjoyments. The quotation, "Man never is, but always to be blest," might, we think, be altered, and contain quite as much truth if it were put thus—Man never is, but always *has been* blest. Do we not all look back to our school-time with delightful and pleasant recollections? These were the halcyon days. Who can describe them without emotion? Boyhood is the fresh spring-time of life. The world was bright and beautiful to us all; we required no exciting pleasures or sensational stimulants to give life a zest—it was a deep joy simply to live; with glowing cheek, and bounding pulse, and buoyant heart, we were in sympathy with Nature, and were happier than kings. The recollection of school-days is a theme which makes the old man eloquent, and which recalls sweet and tender reminiscences to us all. How pleasant it is, while sitting, as we are now, in the close and dusty city, to dream for a moment of the days of our boyhood! In imagination we smell the hawthorn; we see the village green; there is the schoolhouse at the corner, with its diamond-paned windows; the door is open, and we hear the hum and babel of childish voices, and the voice of "The Maister," in the old familiar tones, loud over all.

Alas! this is only a dream. Where are the children now—"the old familiar faces?" Scattered to all points of the compass—some are dead. We can only trace a few. One, who "grasped the skirts of happy chance," is in a high position in the State; another, who seemed cleverer than he,

> " Still ploughs with pain his native lea, .
> And reaps the labour of his hands,
> Or in the furrow musing stands :
> ' Does my old friend remember me ?' "

And what of "The Maister?" We can scarcely think of him now without a smile. We remember the fearful awe of him in which we stood. With his long-tailed coat, peering specs, and twirling tawse, he was a terror to evil-doers. Joseph Teenan has described him well :—

> " His plump roon' cheeks as red's the rose,
> His twinklin' een an' redder nose,
> Showed that he suppit mair than brose—
> > The Maister !

C

" He opened aye the schule wi' prayer ;
    An' psalms an' questions gied us mair
    Than what we thocht was proper.there—
                    The Maister !

" It's forty years noo since that day,
    An' Time, wha's besom's aye at play,
    'Mang other things has soopt away—
                    The Maister !"

We must not, however, unduly extend our paper, however pleasant it is to indulge in the outpouring of personal reminiscences. We must suppose now that we have considered the School-boy, and we must give the stage attendant the hint to let the act-drop fall for the second time. It will rise by-and-by on an exceedingly interesting phase of character.

Third.—The Lover.

" And then the Lover,
Sighing like furnace, with a woeful ballad
Made to his mistress' eyebrow."

UR hero has grown under our hands from Infant to School-boy; we left him in our last paper under the care of the dominie. We must represent him now as having passed that stage. He has left the narrow walls where "The Maister" imparted to him what little knowledge he could, to enter a larger school, where, under the severer teaching of experience, he must learn many hard lessons. We must raise the curtain on him while he is undergoing a very fiery trial. We have now—

" The Lover,
Sighing like furnace, with a woeful ballad
Made to his mistress' eyebrow."

How woe-begone the poor fellow looks! And remember this is no sham; our hero is thoroughly in earnest; only he is not quite sane at present— he is madly in love. He heaves a world of sighs —he is thinking of HER, the irresistible SHE, an

angel—an archangel—a divinity. He would kiss
the ground she treads upon—he would be the glove
upon her hand, or the girdle round her waist. He
would, as Goethe says, puff away sun, moon, and
stars for her sake. He would do anything, however
ridiculous, to win her favour. He is enraptured,
captivated, enslaved,—body and mind. "All his
days are trances, and all his nights are dreams."
But we must remember that the explanation of it is
that he is possessed; the little, laughing, dimpled
god Cupid has got hold of him, and is using him
as a bellows—he has blown him up with love until
he is nearly mad. By-and-by the sighing and ridiculous bluster will expend itself; the furnace will
have roared itself out; and the fine gold of pure,
quiet, undemonstrative, but true and earnest love
will be left behind.

Love is a fact. It appears to us a very strange
thing that love between man and woman should be
classed among those subjects which are not to be
spoken about. It is tabooed in society. Old people
never talk about it; it looks as if they scarcely
believed in it, or were ashamed of the fervour of
youth. Young people chaff each other about it,
but cannot speak of it seriously "before folk." Yet
both old and young know about this love—they

quite understand that when good and true, it is one of the sweetest experiences, best influences, and purest joys of life. We have heard of mammas who never speak of the gentle passion; but in the most proper of ways they can sometimes afford, quite unintentionally, an opportunity for a quiet *tête-à-tête* when an "eligible" appears. And, ah! what declarations have been made by the young people on these occasions! What was said was only intended for one listener. We are not going to make any revelations of our own experience in this matter;—*somebody* might object, you know; but, from what we have seen, we have come to the conclusion that the kind of underhand way in which love-making is so often conducted is a mistake. The thing might appear more openly, and yet all things be done decently and in order.

Love is not often written about in essays, or lectured about from the platform. The subject is entirely left to the novelist; and that is undoubtedly one reason why young people—young ladies, in particular—devour so much of the mawkish, sentimental trash which is daily being discharged from the press. We cannot blame the girls. What is a woman's life without love? People read of that which interests them; and, if love is one great

subject of interest, and it is only treated of by
the novelist, novels will continue to be largely
read.

But what, after all, is this love, which is so great
an element in our life, and bulks so largely in our
thoughts? Can we give an explanation of it? Can
it be defined, tabulated, brought to book, as it
were? Well, we are not metaphysical or philosophical enough to attempt that. All that we can
say is—and we are not at all ashamed to own it—
we know. We would give a woman's reason for the
existence of love—it is so, because it is so; and
should anybody doubt that—

> " A warmth within the breast would melt
>   The freezing reason's colder part,
>   And, like a man in wrath, the heart
>   Would rise and answer, 'I have felt!'"

We should think many of our readers will require
little explanation of the matter, and those who know
nothing of it may probably find out before long.
My dear reader, whose heart is quite untrammelled,
you will, perhaps, turn a corner some day, or enter
a room, and there, before your nose, is the other
half of you. You may not recognise that fact at
the first glance—although some people do—but it
will dawn upon you by-and-by. You will draw closer

and closer. A look, a whisper, a laugh, a gentle pressure of the hand, and there you are. You will doubtless go mad for a time; but the lunacy will pass off. And let us trust that, when you awake in your right mind, you will have acquired a love which will wear well in this matter-of-fact world—a love which will not come out in the washing, but last as well as that of the wife of "John Anderson my Jo," who loved her old husband's frosty pow as much as she had loved her young one's raven locks.

We need not attempt to give any advice about the choosing of people possessing certain qualities. Advice is often the cheapest and most useless commodity. One word only. Equality is a good thing —something like equality in age, education, and social position. There is sometimes a great deal too much importance attached to good looks. Remember Henry V.'s remarks :—" Take a fellow of plain and uncoined constancy. What ! a speaker is but a prater; a rhyme is but a ballad. A good leg will fall; a straight back will stoop; a black beard will turn white; a curled pate will grow bald; a fair face will wither; a full eye will wax hollow; but a good heart, Kate, is the sun and the moon; or, rather, the sun, and not the moon; for it shines bright and never changes, but keeps its course truly."

Love, like blows, is a thing which it is better to give than to receive. Rochefoucauld (Maxim 78) says :—" The pleasure of love is in loving. We are happier in the passion we feel than in that we excite." Or, as Shelley has very beautifully expressed the same sentiment—

> " All love is sweet,
> Given or returned.   Common as light is love,
> And its familiar voice wearies not ever.
> They who inspire it most are fortunate,
> But those who feel it most are happier still."

Samuel Smiles says :—" It is by means of this divine passion that the world is kept ever fresh and young. It is the perpetual melody of humanity. It sheds an effulgence upon youth, and throws a halo round age. It glorifies the present by the light it casts backward, and it lightens the future by the beams it casts forward. Love tends to emancipate the soul from the slavery of self. It inspires gentleness, sympathy, mutual faith, and confidence." The poet Browning says that " all love renders wise in a degree." What appears to us to be one of the finest influences of the gentle passion is, that it takes a man out of himself; the admiration with which you are inspired for another makes you so far self-forgetful ; as some one has said—we forget who—

"Love is the triumph of the unselfish over the selfish part of our nature :"—

"Love took up the harp of Life, and smote on all the chords
    with might—
Smote the chord of Self, that, trembling, pass'd in music
    out of sight."

We might quote many beautiful and true sayings and verses about love ; but that would not be of much use :—

"I waste my heart in signs ; let be. My bride,
My wife, my life. Oh ! we will walk this world,
Yoked in all exercise of noble end,
And so thro' those dark gates across the wild
That no man knows. Indeed I love thee ; come,
Yield thyself up ; my hopes and thine are one ;
Accomplish thou my manhood and thyself;
Lay thy sweet hands in mine, and trust to me."

These very beautiful and sweet lines from Tennyson's "Princess" refer to the more quiet and subdued love of married life. Shakespeare's terse and pithy lines represent the violent and ridiculous side of the outbreak of love in the very young lover.

There is a kind of love termed *calf-love.* If we were writing a book, we might devote a chapter to the consideration of that very curious phenomenon ; but, as our space here will not permit, we must pass it over.

We have referred to the love of young folk who

are not married, but certainly going to be, some fine day; we have also mentioned the more solid and quiet love of married life. But we must remember that love is not confined to these classes. What about our kind old maids and jolly bachelors? We confess to a liking for old maiden ladies, and old bachelors are generally good company. We will pardon them for their unhappy condition if they can produce a good excuse. And what is the excuse which they often could make, but do not like to mention?—a disappointment in love. So then, old maids, who have perhaps too often the same cause to assign, and old bachelors, know as much about love as ourselves. Ah! who knows? Very likely the sourest and most old-maidish of maiden aunts has some soft spot in her withered heart, and many tender memories in her brain. She may have a packet of old faded letters in her tidy escritoire there, over which, when nobody sees, she may shed a regretful tear. And that old port-wine-faced bachelor, with his bald head and silver snuff-box, may have some wonderful romance hidden under his capacious waist-coat. He was once twenty-two. We know one who has a very beautiful little auburn curl folded up as tenderly as if it were gold-leaf, and locked carefully away.

Punch said—" To those who are about to marry —don't." Would it not be as wise a thing to say— To those who are about to *flirt*—don't? Love is not a laughing matter, it is a serious affair; and to make love "in fun" is a very dangerous sport. Many a fair life has been shipwrecked by that. Unrequited love has often been " the worm i' the bud "—

> " The little pitted speck in garnered fruit
>   That, rotting inward, slowly moulders all."

We will not say anything more about this, but trust that our readers have both more heart and sense than indulge in anything like a flirtation, which is serious, and might make mischief.

We must let the curtain down now upon our Lover, and extinguish his sighs. We cannot give him any help in the way of hints how to make love, neither can we assist our readers at all in the matter, however much of a friend we may be to them.

> " Friendship is constant in all other things
>   Save in the office and affairs of love :
>   Therefore, all hearts in love use their own tongues :
>   Let every eye negotiate for itself,
>   And trust no agent."

Fourth.—The Soldier.

" Then, a Soldier
Full of strange oaths, and bearded like the pard ;
Jealous in honour, sudden and quick in quarrel,
Seeking the bubble reputation
Even in the cannon's mouth."

WE prophesied for the Infant, of whom we wrote in our first paper, that time would work the wonders for him which it has done for all of us. Our baby grew into the School-boy, and from the school-boy became the Lover. We have now to consider him at a more advanced stage. What strides he has made ! The weak arms of the babe have become the bands of a man — "the thews that throw the world." The child lay passive in the nurse's arms— he was fragile, delicate, and tender ; now he is erect and strong, with a front like Jove, and with eyes towards heaven ; he is the image of a god.

The child " spake as a child, understood as a child, thought as a child ;" but now he has put away all childish things—he has become A MAN. " What a piece of work is a man ! How noble in reason ! how infinite in faculty! in form and moving, how express and admirable! in action, how like an angel! in apprehension, how like a god!" There is no grander title than this—He is *a man.* A true, strong, earnest, sincere man is the crowning glory of creation. Knights and lords are but the breath of kings—kings themselves are only the creatures of circumstance. "An honest man's the noblest work of God." The Scriptures tell us to "honour all men," and we ought to respect the common humanity which even the poorest and vilest share with us; but we honour men doubly who are men indeed, and the more manly a man is he will stand the higher in our estimation. A nobleman, in the correct sense, is a man who is noble,—who is true, upright, honourable, and strong. "The glory of a young man is his strength." He must be strong in intellect to know—strong in will and muscle to perform.

As men admire the gentle, tender, affectionate nature of women, so women admire the strong and powerful character of men. It is man's duty to grapple; it is woman's to embrace.

Our hero, in whom we are very much interested, and we hope our readers also, has grown out of the *dilettante,* sickly, sentimental state in which we left him in our last paper. He was sighing like a furnace

—he was madly in love, writing sonnets to show that the most perfectly beautiful thing in all the world was his sweetheart's eyebrow.   With shoe untied, and hair unkempt, in a general state of *négligé*, his eyes in a wild frenzy rolling, he was well laughed at, although we secretly sympathised with him too.   But now the scene is changed.   " Young Harry has his beaver on, his cuisses on his thighs, gallantly armed."   Hurrah for the transformation !   We prefer the clink of spurs to the jingle of rhyme, and the tramp of armed men to the cadence of measured verses.   Our Lover has given up sighing ; he will make no more woeful ballads. As the lion wooes his bride, so will he ; and he has a better chance of success by the change of tactics. Desdemona was true to her sex when she loved Othello for the dangers he had passed.   A Hercules or a Samson is more likely to win ladies' favours than the delicate, elegant, " spoony " kind of man.   The curled darlings of the *salon*, who can rhyme themselves into ladies' good graces, and " have cunning in pro-testation," cannot rival the strong, brave, true-hearted Soldier, who, like the one we are now considering, is—

> " Full of strange oaths, and bearded like the pard ;
> Jealous in honour, sudden and quick in quarrel,
> Seeking the bubble reputation .
> Even in the cannon's mouth."

We all love the Soldier—why? Because he is the man *par excellence.* He is honourable, open, true, and brave. He is simply just as Shakespeare has painted him.

There is a romance about the profession of arms that charms all of us, and fascinates women in particular. There was a time when all men were soldiers, and every woman a soldier's wife or daughter. In those days the hearth had to be protected by the sword, and it was necessary that "a strong man armed should keep the house." The only way to a woman's heart at that time was by the exhibition of deeds of prowess. The knight at the tournament threw down his gauntlet, declaring his lady to be the fairest of the fair; and he stood to his averment, and attempted to prove it by killing, if possible, everybody who dared to deny it.

Now-a-days, of course, matters are different, and it is better that they should be. All men are not soldiers; but we civilians should remember that it is to the Soldier we are indebted for the liberties we enjoy. This is a very matter-of-fact age; all men except the Soldier seem engaged in a fierce race for wealth :—

> " For gold the merchant ploughs the main,
>   The farmer ploughs the manor ;
>   But glory is the sodger's prize,
>   The sodger's wealth is honour."

Surely our country, with all its grand history, will never learn to despise its soldiery, or to hold as a small matter the glory and honour which is the soldier's only reward. Here is a letter from Florence Nightingale on the subject, in which she cites some instances of noble hardihood. We shall take the liberty of quoting from it :—

"England, from her grand mercantile and commercial successes, has been called sordid ; God knows she is not. The simple courage, the enduring patience, the good sense, the strength to suffer in silence—what nation shows more of this in war than is shown by her commonest soldier ? I have seen men dying of dysentery, but, scorning to report themselves sick lest they should thereby throw more labour on their comrades, go down to the trenches and make the trenches their death-bed. There is nothing in history to compare with it. . . . Say what men will, there is something more truly Christian in the man who gives his time, his strength, his life, if need be, for something not himself—whether he call it his Queen, his country, or his colours—than in all the asceticism, the fasts, the humiliations, and confessions which have ever been made ; and this spirit of giving one's life, without calling it a sacrifice, is found nowhere as truly as in England."

Old John Falstaff said of honour, " Can honour set a leg ? no ; or an arm ? no ; or take away the grief of a wound ? no ;"—and therefore he would have none of it. Let us be thankful that everybody is not of Falstaff's opinion. We know what honour is, and give it willingly to the noble and the brave. We saw in the newspapers the other day that a distinguished and wealthy lord, in presenting a medal to a private of the Forty-Second Highlanders — our own brave Black Watch—for his courage at the taking of Coomassie, said he would willingly give all he possessed to stand in the shoes of the poor recipient.

We must not, however, weary our readers with a dissertation upon honour, but return to the consideration of our Soldier. Shakespeare says he is "jealous in honour, sudden and quick in quarrel." We are not to understand by this that he is very quarrelsome, and has pleasure in angry dispute. No, no! He is neither a rowdy nor a bully. Being honest and honourable, he is quick in repudiating any charge against his good name; and, being a soldier, he cannot talk himself out of a difficulty;—he does not know how to apologise, and blows come readier to him than words.

We approve of, and admire, the Christian principle of patience and long-suffering; but at the same time we can sympathise with the man who will not pocket a deliberate insult. Perhaps this sympathy is an indication of the strength of the old Adam in us; but we do not believe it. We cannot be expected to submit quietly to every injustice, and, like "Uriah Heep," to smile and be very 'umble in all circumstances.

Our Soldier is brave; "he seeks the bubble reputation even in the cannon's mouth." We will not
attempt to describe him in action, or regale our readers
with the horrors of some desperate and bloody encoun-
ter. We might imagine him leading some forlorn
hope, amid the yell of onset, the boom of cannon,
the clash of steel, the shrieks of the dying; we could
think of him rushing up the scaling ladder, bespattered
with blood, and in the very teeth of death planting
his colours on some conquered battlement; we might
suppose him one of the gallant Six Hundred who
charged at Balaclava—

> " Cannon to right of them,
> Cannon to left of them,
> Cannon in front of them,
>   Volleyed and thundered.
> Stormed at with shot and shell,
> Boldly they rode and well,
> Into the jaws of Death,
> Into the mouth of Hell,
>   Rode the Six Hundred.

> " Flashed all their sabres bare,
> Flashed as they turned in air,
> Sabring the gunners there,
> Charging an army, while
>   All the world wondered :
> Plunged in the battery smoke,
> Right through the line they broke,

Cossack and Russian
Reeled from the sabre-stroke,
   Shattered and sundered.
Then they rode back, but not—
   Not the Six Hundred."

We might make the last line of this verse a subject for remark—" Not the Six Hundred." Thousands have sought the bubble reputation at the cannon's mouth, and only found death, their reward being an unknown grave in a distant land. The pride, pomp, and circumstance of war may be pleasant things to dwell upon, but these are only tinsel trappings ; take the gilt off, and there is something very hideous below. We could quote most harrowing descriptions of the battle-field, both during and after the battle; and the most graphic of these give but a very faint idea of the scene. Let those who wish to read such, turn up Dr. Russell's letters from the Crimea, when he was there as correspondent for the *Times*. Yet, after all, we need not go so far back. The newspapers published during the late Franco-Prussian war contain quite enough, and the newspapers which will be published during the next war that may take place will tell the same tale. The reporter's office is a strange one now-a-days. He sits very quietly in the gallery allotted to him in the House of Commons, taking down the speeches which are gradually leading up to a war. He marks the smooth sinuosities, the sublimely vague terminology, the endless coilings of sleek diplomacy; and when the word-fight is over, when other combatants step upon the platform—the warriors, whose battle is with confused noise and garments rolled in blood—the reporter becomes "war correspondent." He goes to the field of action, and takes notes, and prints them. He steps about among the dead and dying, and telegraphs the latest news.

My dear young reader, whose head is full of the romance of war, just read some of these accounts, and you will get a dim notion of the reality of it. And you, young ladies, who have *scarlet* fever, and "doat on the military," perhaps it would do you good also to get some true idea of the real evils of war.

We may all very fervently pray for the time when war shall be no more, and the shedding of blood cease; —the milder, yet more truly heroic, time when all that high courage, that noble daring, that unimpeachable honour, that strong arm, that contempt of death, that admirable love of country which characterise the true soldier, shall be no longer wasted on such brutal and bloody purposes, but consecrated to do battle with moral and spiritual evil within and without—in self, society, and the state. We can all be soldiers in this warfare, and surely there can be no better, no nobler outlet for the energies of rational and immortal beings.

So much, then, for our Soldier. When the curtain of our theatre rose, the orchestra played "See the Conquering Hero comes." We must now sound the trumpet, beat the drums, screw up the fiddles, play " God save the Queen," and let the act-drop fall.

Fifth.—The Justice.

> " And then the Justice,
> In fair round belly with good capon lined ;
> With eyes severe, and beard of formal cut,
> Full of wise saws and modern instances ;
> And so he plays his part."

THE Baby, the School-boy, the Lover, the Soldier —these are the four Ages which we have already considered. Round goes the world ; the whirligig of time revolves a little longer ; a few years slip away, and the Soldier is a soldier no more ; he is the same man, but a different character. The lapse of time has this effect upon us all. Physiologists tell us that our bodies even are undergoing perpetual change, and that the whole man is renewed from top to toe in a certain number of years ; so that, in fact, that nose of yours is not the same nose that you had seven years ago, and your head is thoroughly changed both inside and out.

Is it not a proof of the duality of our existence that we use the word " my " when we say my head, my heart, my arm, &c. ? What is the *me* to which all these things belong ? These members are all

changing, yet the *me* remains the same. Philosophers have puzzled themselves and others about
what they call *the me*, and the *not me*—the *ego*, and
the *non ego;* and yet they know no more about it
than the simplest reader of this paper. We do not
require a knowledge of metaphysics to know ourselves from anybody else ; the stupidest person will
not lose himself in a crowd, or forget his own
identity. Time makes great changes upon us all,
and yet with all these changes we are, to use a
common expression, "the same, but different." We
have different ideas in the same mind, and we have
always the same spirit inhabiting a body which is
marked by time.

The difference in a man's personal appearance at
the various stages of life is very great. Very quietly
and silently the years mark us, and we go about
bearing on our faces proofs of our age more reliable,
perhaps, than any extract from a register. Could
the boy of ten years of age see a *carte* of himself
when he shall have grown to manhood's estate, he
certainly would not know himself; and could the
lover of sixteen, with incipient moustache and the
rosy bloom of youth upon his cheek, get a glimpse
of himself as he will look at sixty, he would mourn
for the metamorphosis.

In our last paper we had—

> "The Soldier,
> Full of strange oaths, and bearded like the pard."

A change has now come over the spirit of his dream. He has trimmed his beard, and given up the strange oaths. The bubble reputation which he sought so strenuously, "even in the cannon's mouth," is not quite so great a thing now in his estimation as it was then. He would rather be considered wise than brave ; and as for any scaling-ladder feats, and leading forlorn hopes—that was well enough for the impetuous Soldier. There is a difference in the physique now, which forbids any such violent exertions. The Soldier has become an eminently respectable middle-aged gentleman. Carlyle may laugh at a man's respectability being gauged by the fact that he keeps a gig, but we come to the conclusion that this man is respectable from the fact of his holding so important an office. We may have a look at him, and as he sits in public we may enter when we choose ; we shall wipe our feet at the door, appear hat in hand, and be very circumspect. There he is on the bench—

> "The Justice,
> In fair round belly with good capon lined ;
> With eyes severe, and beard of formal cut,
> Full of wise saws and modern instances ;
> And so he plays his part."

One day, not very long ago, in a country town, we walked into a Sheriff-Court to take notes for a minute. The Court was held in a little dirty room. The Sheriff-Substitute of a certain county was on the bench ; a paltry small debt case was being heard. A pursuer, a defender, two or three witnesses, a sheriff-officer, and ourselves were all who were present. Here is what took place during the few minutes of our stay :—

" Silence in the Court," growled the hungry-looking sheriff-officer.

The defender, a woman, seemed to be continuing a harangue begun before our entrance. Addressing the respectable Sheriff-Substitute, she said, " My lord, yes, my lord, as I said before, says I, says she to me, it was a week past on Wednesday, I mind it was an awfu' wat day, and Betsy M'Neil's coo——"

" My good woman," replied the Justice, dangling his eye-glass—and a fine, jolly, red-faced man he was—" you are irrelevant."

The severe look which accompanied the remark, coupled with the woman's ignorance of the meaning of the word irrelevant, fairly frightened her. She seemed reassured, however, when, with a kindly smile, " my lord " (who was no lord at all) urged her to be brief.

"Leave Betsy M'Neil's *coo* alone, woman," said he. "Stick to the point, be short, be brief; brevity, you know, is the soul of wit."

"Ah ha!" we said (*into ourselves*, you know, for we were afraid of the sheriff-officer),—"here is the Justice with his wise saws; we will take the liberty of quizzing him a little, and will describe him as he sits there." His face is both long and broad, if that is not a contradiction in terms. His black beard is cut square, like a boxwood-hedge. His eyes, overhung by bushy iron-grey eyebrows, look exceedingly fierce and stern; but the "eye severe" does not overawe one too much, as it is evident the look is put on, and the rest of the countenance will not bear it out. These round full cheeks of his have not certainly a "vinegar aspect," and his nose, which he is colouring as carefully as a smoker does a meerschaum, declares him at once to be no unfrequent participator at the social board. He looks quite like a justice of the old school; knee-breeches and buckled shoes would complete the thing. He has the round stomach, the old-fashioned waist-coat, the dangling seals, and the double-barrelled eye-glasses. He looks pleased with himself, some-what in the way a fine cropper-pigeon does. But it will not do for him to show too much of the *suaviter in modo.* He must be a terror to evil-doers, and therefore he looks severe; he must be considered wise, and therefore he airs his "saws and modern instances;" and so he plays his part.

This is a very different character from the rash, strong-headed, impetuous Soldier whom we saw in our last paper. Shakespeare did not say of *him*, "and so he plays his part;" neither was the remark made about the sighing Lover, the lazy School-boy, or the crying Infant. Why, then, is it thrown in after the description of the Justice? The reason, we think, is this—that although each of the other characters acted a part, yet the Justice is the only one conscious that he is so acting. The Lover was ridiculously sincere, the Soldier was fearfully in earnest, but the Justice is more cool than either of these. He has taken the bearing of things, and has a due regard for what are called "the proprieties." The natural man has grown into the conventional citizen. We do not mean to bring a charge of insincerity against the worthy Justice; all that we mean to say is, that he is a stringent observer of the laws of society. Like every one of us, he must reverence the code of which some mythical person named Mrs. Grundy is the Solon. He must support the dignity of his office by looking severe; he must be witty and wise, so he quotes proverbs. His beard even is of formal cut. It is not proper for him to use any more strange oaths, so he has given these up, except on very special occasions. Now that he is a Justice, he must, to use a good homely expression, "behave himself before folk "—

"And so he plays his part;"

while, perhaps, as a man he finds this part-playing a little irksome to him.

Might the same remark which is made about this Justice not be made about almost everybody who has reached the same time of life? The Infant does nothing for the sake of effect, and it has not the slightest respect for decorum; what it wants to do, that it does, without regard to what people may think. When a child is tired of you, it soon lets you know it; it cannot smile, and look happy, and be delighted to see you, and yet at the same time wish you far enough away. The School-boy cannot dissemble his love or hate. The Lover cares not how ridiculous he may appear in the eyes of others so long as "he pleases his love." It is not every Soldier who cares so much for appearance as to arrange his uniform, as the Roman did his toga, before he falls. But the man who has passed through these stages, to what is he not the slave?

He is the bondsman of habit, fashion, prejudice, propriety. He cannot be a law unto himself, and do what is right in his own eyes; but he must make the opinion of a great number of other people the law of his life. It is not only necessary to do at Rome as Rome does, but we must do everywhere what everybody does. We do not wish to be cynical or severe, or to write a woeful book of lamentations about the degeneracy of the times. We will not cry, as Hamlet did—

> " The time is out of joint ; O cursed spite !
> That ever I was born to set it right."

But surely we might be allowed to hint that this extreme submission to the laws of custom is a grievance, and it would be a good thing if some strong-minded leader in society would break up and abolish many of its conventional rules and distinctions. Like the poor, silly, old, affected, painted woman in " Dombey and Son," we wish most earnestly that people would be more natural. We should not think so much about " what will people say, what will people think, how will this look." We should do what we think right, whatever may be the opinion of others. It would not be wrong to break through any of these restrictions of society if we thought proper; but it is somewhat difficult to do it. Every circle and section, set and clique, has its own laws, which must be obeyed at the risk of expulsion from the coterie. A popular writer says :— "Some men are immured within a bastile of fashion, others of custom, others of opinion; and few there are who have the courage to think outside their sect, to act outside their party, and to step into the free air of individual thought and action. We dress and eat and follow fashion, though it may be at the risk of debt, ruin, and misery; living, not so much according to our means, as according to the superstitious observance of our class. Though we may speak contemptuously of Indians who flatten their heads, and of the Chinese who cramp their toes, we have only to look at the deformities of fashion among ourselves to see that the reign of Mrs. Grundy is universal."

In future we mean to pay as little heed as possible to that old lady potentate. It is surely the best plan to make our own conscience the guide of action. As Sir Harry Wotton has beautifully written :—

> " How happy is he born and taught,
>   That serveth not another's will ;
>   Whose armour is his honest thought,
>   And simple truth his utmost skill !

> " Whose passions not his masters are,
>   Whose soul is still prepared for death,
>   Untied unto the world by care
>   Of public fame or private breath.

*   *   *   *

" This man is freed from servile bands
   Of hope to rise, or fear to fall;
Lord of himself, though not of lands,
   He having nothing, yet hath all."

We think we hear some reader say that this tirade about custom and fashion is all very good, but what has it to do with "The Justice?" Should any theologian think that this our lay sermon is not textual, we beg to differ from him;—it is all in the words, "and so he plays his part." It must not be thought for a moment that the good, jolly Justice is a man of shams. By no means! Honesty is written on his face, sociality depicted on his nose; but still the Justice as a justice does pretend a little, and would fain throw dust in our eyes.

It is time now, however, that we bow ourselves out of Court. The sheriff-officer has his eye upon us. The Sheriff is going home to dinner, and so are we; and, depend upon it, the Justice will do justice to his victuals.

SIXTH.—THE PANTALOON.

> " The sixth age shifts
> Into the lean and slippered Pantaloon,
> With spectacles on nose, and pouch on side ;
> His youthful hose well saved, a world too wide
> For his shrunk shank ; and his big, manly voice,
> Turning again toward childish treble, pipes
> And whistles in his sound."

THE curtain is up again, and with a whoop and halloo a strange quartette rushes upon the stage—the columbine, harlequin, clown, and pantaloon.

It is the last of the four with whom we have to do. Look at him, poor old boy. He needs a stick to walk with, spectacles to see with, and slippers for his gouty toes. He has a strange cough, too ; but withal there is a good deal of " go " in him yet—he is no melancholy Jaques, and is as fond of fun as ever. This is the pantaloon of the pantomime, who is only a very broad caricature of the Pantaloon of real life. (We accept the word, since it is Shakespeare's.)

In our last paper we had the Justice under our hands. He was jolly, happy, and in good condition ;

but time has changed him since then. As Shakespeare very expressively says, he has " shifted " into a more advanced stage. The change has come very gradually. Medical men tell us that there is a certain time of life when the old man quite changes his constitution, and becomes thin and pale instead of stout and hearty. At fifty many men present the appearance our Justice did ; but at seventy the description of Shakespeare's Pantaloon is usually more correct.

The proverb " Laugh and grow fat" is so well known that we are apt to think that lean people are bound to be melancholy and sour ; and yet we all know that this is not the case. Our subject, for instance— " the Pantaloon "—we will call him old man in future —is not crusty and disagreeable ; he is as happy as most people. We will refuse to believe that old men, as a class, are more melancholy than any other ; because from our own experience we know they are not so. We·are acquainted with old men who are the best of company ; and yet there are exceptions to this, as to every other rule. Perhaps it was an exception whom Shakespeare had in his eye, for it must be admitted that the account given of the appearance of the old man is far from being very cheerful :—

" With spectacles on nose, and pouch on side ;
His youthful hose well saved, a world too wide

E

> For his shrunk shank ; and his big manly voice
> Turning again towards childish treble, pipes
> And whistles in its sound."

We know there are old men who are querulous and cross, and have no happiness in life; their power of enjoyment is for ever gone. The lives of such men will not stand much examination. Thackeray describes well the miserable existence of an old rake. He has played out his part, and is only alive to repent and mourn. We pity such a character. Like King Lear, he is a poor, infirm, weak, and despised old man, and he has only himself to blame. He may say with the poet—

> " My days are in the yellow leaf,
>   The flowers and fruits of love are gone ;
> The worm, the canker, and the grief
>   Are mine alone ! "

The French have a word *désillusionné*, disillusioned. This word accurately applies to such a man. He thinks all happiness an illusion. Hain Friswell, the author of the " Gentle Life," has beautifully written on this subject, and has thus described the jaded sensualist :—" He has been behind the scenes, and has seen the bare walls of the theatre, without the light and the paint, and has watched the ugly actors and gaunt actresses by daylight. The taste of life is very bitter in the mouth of such a man; his joys are

Dead Sea apples—dust and ashes in the mouths of those who bite them. No flowers spring up about his path; he is very melancholy and suspicious, very hard and incredulous; he has faith neither in the honesty of man nor in the purity of woman. He is *désillusionné* —by far too wise to be taken in with painted toys. Every one acts with self-interest! his doctor, his friend, or his valet, will be sorry for his death, merely from the amount of money-interest that they have in his life. Bare and grim unto tears, even if he had any, is the life of such a man. With him sadder than Lethe or the Styx, the river of time runs between stony banks, and, often a calm suicide, it bears him to the Morgue. Happier by far is he who, with whitened hair and wrinkled brow, sits crowned with the flowers of illusion; and who, with the ear of age, still remains a charmed listener to the songs which pleased his youth, trusting ' his heart and what the world calls illusions.' "

We say, however, that this style of old man is not a fair type of the class. It would be a miserable thing indeed if that were the case. It would not be worth while living this life, if the only outcome of it all was that the *Vanitas Vanitatum* of the preacher was the only truth.

Old age may in many cases be happier than youth. All the wild fervour of youth has passed away; all strong endeavour and feverish ambition has died out. The old man is calm, and still, and quiet. He has done what he can. He has many pleasant memories; doubtless he has had many disappointments; he has known joy and sorrow. " His mind to him a kingdom is."

Life is for the most part but the mirror of our own individual selves. Our mind gives to all situations, to all fortunes, high or low, their real characters. To the good the world is good; to the bad it is bad. If our views of life be elevated—if we regard it as a sphere of useful effort, of high living and high thinking, of working for others' good as well as our own—then we may look forward to a serene old age, which will be joyful, hopeful, and blessed.

Pardon us, kind reader, for this little sermonette : that the subject has a serious side you will readily perceive. We hope that when you and ourselves come to the time of life at which Shakespeare indicates the Pantaloon to have arrived, we shall be happier than he supposes him to be. If we are lean, may it be only the effect of time ; if we are slippered, let us hope kind hands sewed for us the slippers we shall shuffle about in ; if our voice become a childish treble, may we have sympathetic and loving friends to listen to its tone ; and if our hose be well saved, let us suppose it is from our preference for the old rather than from an inability to acquire the new.

What we wish to lay before our readers is this fact, that, whatever Shakespeare may suppose, old age is often a very happy time; and that, whether ours shall turn out to be happy or not, very much depends upon our conduct now. We ourselves have one intimate friend, about eighty years of age, whose jokes are richer and his laughter more hearty than those of many men three score years his junior. When rheumatism twinges through his shrunk shanks he positively laughs, and cries, with a comical face, " Ha, ha, ha, there it is again! He, he! isn't that curious?" He can tell fine old stories in his tremulous voice, about "the days o' auld langsyne." Like all old men, his mind dwells constantly in the past. Young people look forward—the world is before them. Old people delight in retrospect—the world is all behind. About one's future nobody knows much—it is the undiscovered country.

We said that the old man was still and quiet; his period of action and active adventure was over. That is not always the case. We see many men as active at eighty as they were at eighteen. Just look around for proof. Take our own Houses of Parliament, for instance; the greatest, most active, and most useful men in both have got up to, or passed, the allotted three score years and ten. Look at our leading judges in the Court of Session in Edinburgh, or the professors in our Universities. You will find, perhaps, that a majority of the greatest men in literature, art, and science are old men. These men are strong giants—not shrivelled pantaloons. In history we find many instances of great energy exhibited at a great age. Wellington planned and superintended the erection of fortifications at eighty. Bacon, Humboldt, and Brewster were fine old students; and the work which they performed at an advanced age could certainly not have been so well performed when they were in all the vigour of youth. It has been said that experience teaches fools; but they showed what it teaches wise men. Although Shakespeare makes the typical old man in "The Seven Ages" a somewhat melancholy-looking character, he has few old men in his plays really like the Pantaloon. Old men are often the happiest and most amusing, according to Shakespeare's own showing. Take, for instance, Old Montague, Capulet, Friar Lawrence, Falstaff, &c. Young Hamlet was melancholy-mad—old Polonius is full of fine humour and wise maxims.

"Old and ugly" are words which are very often coupled together. We do not see why they should be so. An old tree may be the most beautiful in the forest; an old cathedral the finest edifice in the city; an old bridge the most beautiful feature in a landscape. And the old men, the white-bearded patriarchs, have their own beauty. "The hoary head is a crown of glory."

" Old and wise "—these are the words that should go together. We should show age the reverence which is its due. When we ourselves see a very old man leaning upon the top of his staff, we sometimes feel inclined to take off our hat to him. Surely he quite as much deserves this courteous and outward token of respect as that pert little boarding-school miss tripping past there with her nose in the air; and she claims this as her due. We mean no offence to the young ladies by this remark, and hope we have not given any.

This is an age, it appears to us, in which there is very little manifestation of reverence or respect for anything under the sun. Our most sacred institutions are criticised with a freedom which would have astonished the last generation. The desire and plea-sure of the ancient Athenians consisted in hearing and telling something new. Our own time seems possessed with the same spirit, and with this addition, that there is something more than talking—the speech is developed into action. All our affairs, both ecclesiastical and political, are in a state of transition and change,—of what the philosophers call *becoming.* Yet, after all, we might do much worse in some cases than stick to the old. As Goldsmith says, " I love everything that's old—old friends, old times, old manners, old books, old wine."

Had we not declared to ourselves that in writing these papers we would never attempt to give any advice —that is always a thankless and useless proceeding—we might here have exhorted young men to "give honour to whom honour is due," and reminded them that old age is honourable. It has been remarked that young men think old men fools, and that old men know young men to be so. This is rather a disagreeable and ill-natured remark, but it contains undoubtedly a little truth. Old men are occasionally apt to be prosy and egotistical—to tell the same story over and over again ; they continually dwell on old times—the good old days of sixty years ago. It should not require much patience to bear with these little things.

The idea of growing old seems to be one which many people put as far away from their minds as possible ; and yet if we sit down and seriously consider the matter, the prospect is not so very unpleasant as we imagine. It only requires to be looked in the face, and, like many other bugbears, the unpleasantness of the idea will vanish. Charles Lamb writes delightfully of his own experience, when as an old man he had to retire from his office. He says that during a busy and active life the time is not our own. It was only after he was superannuated that he felt he could do what he liked; and the days and hours were longer then and more precious to him than during his busy manhood. His experience is probably the experience of many. Look around, and you will see very many happy old men. Few of them perhaps would care to live over their lives again, beginning at childhood and having exactly the same experiences twice. They are contented as they are, and we need not be at all afraid of that which pleases them. William Cullen Bryant very quietly contemplates the time when he will be an old man, in the verses which we quote; why should each of us not be able to cherish similar feelings?

" Lament who will, in fruitless tears,
    The speed with which our moments fly,
  I sigh not over vanished years,
    But watch the years that hasten by.

" Look how they come ! a mingled crowd
    Of bright and dark, but rapid days ;
  Beneath them, like a summer cloud,
    The wide world changes as I gaze.

" Time, time will seam and blanch my brow :
    Well, I will sit with aged men,
And my good glass will tell me how
    A grisly beard becomes me then.

" And should no foul dishonour lie
    Upon my head when I am gray,
Love yet shall watch my fading eye,
    And smooth the path of my decay.

" Then, haste thee, Time—'tis kindness all
    That speeds thy wingéd feet so fast ;
Thy pleasures stay not till they fall,
    And all thy pains are quickly past.

" Thou fliest, and bear'st away our woes,
    And as thy shadowy train depart,
The memory of sorrow grows
    A lighter burden on the heart."

My dear Reader, whether we will or not, we must grow old. There is no shirking the matter. If we remain here, that is a certainty; but yet we need not be alarmed about it. Let us see that we avoid doing anything now which will fill us with unhappy reflections then. We will trust in Providence, and hope we may be spared to enjoy—

" An old age serene and bright,
    And lovely as a Lapland night."

SEVENTH AND LAST.—"SANS EVERYTHING."

> " Last scene of all,
> That ends this strange, eventful history,
> Is second childishness and mere oblivion ;
> Sans teeth, sans eyes, sans taste, sans—everything."

THIS is the last scene of all. What has led up to it? We wrote first of the Infant, who was quite helpless in the nurse's arms. He had a mind and senses, but he was too inexperienced to use them. It might be said of him, as is written about the gods of the heathen, that he had eyes but could not see, ears but could not hear, hands but could not handle, and an understanding that could not understand. The performance of the first Act was only

" The Infant, mewling and puking in the nurse's arms."

Round went the clock, and the curtain rose for the second time. The babe had grown into the boy; he had looked about him, and had begun to know and understand, so he had to present himself at the more advanced stage of

" The School-boy, with his satchel and shining morning face."

We saw him loitering by the burn-side, chasing

butterflies and watching the dappled trout; he was going very unwillingly to school, but it was necessary that he should go. So we left him under the care of the dominie until he developed into

"The Lover, sighing like a furnace."

We laughed at him now, and sympathised with him too, in some measure. We knew he would sigh himself into a quieter and happier condition; and we hoped that, when he did awake, and was in his right mind, he would find himself possessed of a good, true, happy, sober love which would endure "until death." Leaving him to accomplish that all-important matter, we let the act-drop fall; and when it rose on Act IV., it was to the sound of martial music and rolling drums. There rushed upon the stage

"The Soldier, jealous in honour—sudden and quick in quarrel."

He was *the man* — noble, honest, true, and brave. He won his spurs, and, in theatrical parlance, "brought down the house." Hearty, ringing cheers reverberated through the theatre; and the warrior retired, to appear again in a remarkably different character. With all respectful curiosity we watched his appearance and performance in the fifth Act, when

"The Justice, in fair round belly with good capon lined,"

sat upon the bench, looked severe, pretended to be

wise, and, as Shakespeare said, " so played his part."
The jolly Justice then shifted into the character we
considered in our last paper—

"The lean and slippered Pantaloon,"

—the superannuated old man. This brings us to the

" Last scene of all,
That ends this strange, eventful history :
'Tis second childishness and mere oblivion ;
Sans teeth, sans eyes, sans taste, sans—everything."

Truly the history has been strange and eventful,
and yet it is a very common one—it is simply "the
common lot." We drew upon our own experience
in some of the Ages; and in those which we have
not yet reached we only required to look around,
to see at once the very characters whom Shakespeare
so accurately described three hundred years ago.

We have arrived now at something very like the point
at which we started. We began with childhood, and we
end with it again. When the babe was born, the clock
began to tick for him : since then the hands have been
turning round and round, and round and round; and
now they are slowly and surely moving up to the point
at which they shall mark time for the old man no
longer. He has seen and heard; he has lived his life ;
he is full of years; he has gone the whole round of his
existence. And what is it all? Life has been com-

pared to a dream, a vision, a vapour, the grass of the field, the weaver's shuttle. "We spend our years as a tale that is told"—that is perhaps the best image. A monument may last for ages; a book or written history can be grasped. A tale is only breath; the words are fugitive and passing; incident succeeds incident by insensible transitions—some are grave, some gay; and then, when the tale is told, there is nothing left behind; the echoes of the tones of the teller soon pass away, and are forgotten.

We will not allow ourselves, however, to enter into any vain and melancholy regrets about the shortness of life. That is a subject which has elicited a world of groans since time began. However much we may bewail the shortness of life, our own efforts cannot prolong it. We shall never be able to make the moon stand still, as Joshua did at Ajalon; or cause the sun's shadow to fall back, as it did on the dial of Ahaz, in answer to the prayers of the prophet. Our duty is to make a good use of the time we have, and not to sit down moping and mourning over the short-ness of the period which we can call our own.

In these pages we have been considering a life in which there was a great deal of happiness. We do not recollect whether we were very happy as an Infant or not. We all look back with delight to our School-boy days. Who can express the sweet happiness the Lover enjoys? The Justice was a jolly character, who enjoyed a good dinner. The Pantaloon, or more properly the old man, had his own pleasures, as we showed in our last paper; and certainly this very aged man, who has reached the stage of second childhood, has much to be thankful for. Of course there have been trials and afflictions to endure. Life all sunshine without shade, all happiness without sorrow, all pleasure without pain, were not life at all—at least not human life. Take the lot of the happiest, it is a tangled yarn—it is made up of sorrows and joys, and the joys are the sweeter. because of the sorrows; bereavements and blessings, one following another, make us sad and blessed by turns. But life is not a dull, sad, melancholy thing: there is a deal of true happiness in the lot of almost every one. It is more natural, perhaps, to remember the afflictions, and dwell upon the sorrows of life, when one has reached a certain age, than to revert to past pleasures and enjoyments; but that is a tendency which should be checked. Robertson, of Brighton, in speaking of the mingled good and evil in life, and the preponderance of the good over the evil, has beautifully said :—" See two men meeting together on the street,—mere acquaintances. They will not be five minutes together before a smile will overspread their countenances, or a merry laugh ring off at the lowest amusement. This has God done. God created the smile and the laugh, as well as the sigh and the tear. The aspect of this life is stern, very stern. It is a very superficial account of it, which slurs over its grave mystery, and refuses to hear its low, deep, undertone of anguish. But there is enough, from hour to hour, of bright sunny happiness, to remind us that its Creator's name is Love."

We said that the old man whose faculties have all gone done—who has reached second childhood, and who can neither see, hear, nor taste well—has much to be thankful for. Perhaps the reader may think this a bold assertion, and one difficult to establish. It is not so. Shakespeare says of him he is "sans everything"—sans teeth, sans eyes, sans taste. But this superannuated old man is not without everything—he is not without happiness or comfort—he is not without pride, either, for old men are proud of their years, and they have a right to be so.

It is a more easy thing for the old man to resign himself to the dissolution which is before him than for the strong man who may be laid on a bed of sickness in the prime of life. The latter has been stopped, as it were, in the middle of his career, and has to leave much unaccomplished; while the former—the wearied sage—has fought out the life-battle, has sounded all the depths and shoals of existence, and, surrounded by kind and loving friends, he simply bides his time. Nothing excites or disturbs him now; the heat of the conflict is over, and he leaves younger men to pull the oar, or put their shoulders to the wheel.

We have read a play which well exemplifies the state of quiet content into which the old man sinks. There was a scene in it to this effect:—Some dreadful and very afflicting news (about what we forget) was brought to a little cottage; a father, mother, and daughter were all thrown into a great state of weeping and distress; while the old grandfather in the chimney-corner was not concerned at all,—he only troubled himself about his handkerchief and his gruel.

Extreme age comes upon a man very gently; it is like the quiet *gloamin'* of a summer eve. The shadows creep very gradually in. The days of an old man are very long to him, just as a day to a young child seems a much longer time than it does to a grown man. It may seem a hard thing to say, but perhaps after all the old man has reason to be thankful even that his senses are gradually failing. If he was as well able to enjoy all this beautiful world in his old age as he was in his youth, he would feel it a harder thing to tear

F

himself away from it. Yet what can we say of those comforts which old age may enjoy unknown to us? When the gateways of sense are being so slowly closed, may not the inner spirit have communications of which we know nothing?

> " Such harmony is in immortal souls ;
>   But whilst this muddy vesture of decay
>   Doth grossly close it in, we cannot hear it."

This is only a matter of conjecture with us ; but we have seen old men whose happy faces looked as if they had some comfort of which they could not speak.

> " The seas are quiet when the winds give o'er ;
>   So calm are we when passions are no more.
>   For then we know how vain it was to boast
>   Of fleeting things, too certain to be lost ;
>   Clouds of affection from our younger eyes
>   Conceal that emptiness which age descries.

> " The soul's dark cottage, battered and decayed,
>   Lets in new light through chinks that time has made :
>   Stronger by weakness, wiser men·become,
>   As they draw near to their eternal home.
>   Leaving the old, both worlds at once they view,
>   That stand upon the threshold of the new."

Dear Reader, we have now come to the end of our task. We have endeavoured to bring a lesson or two out of this beautiful passage from Shakespeare—" The Seven Ages;" and whether we have been successful or not it is for you to judge. We will not, however, say anything about ourselves. We have our own part to play on the world's stage, and so have you. The part we had to perform in laying before you the Seven Acts of the life which we have just described, was a very simple one. We were only scene-shifter— we pulled the act-drop up and down; so it does not become us to write an epilogue. We must keep out of sight in " the wings;" and now, when the performance is over, our only duty is to put out the lights. We saw good old Dean Ramsay the last time he acted as chairman at a public meeting in Edinburgh; and perhaps we might be allowed to say to you what he said to that great gathering in the Music Hall—

" Guid nicht, an' joy be wi' ye a'."

LYRICS.

LYRICS.

Devotional Pieces.

A PRAYER.

MAY HE,
    Who, through the thunder
  And the noise
Of howling wolfish winds
  At midnight hour,
    Hears, from the wave-washed deck,
The sailor boy's
  Poor feeble cry for help
  When tempests lower,
Protect thy little bark
  On Life's dark sea,
And through the hurricane
  Thy Helmsman be :
  Till, safe within
    The haven of the blest,
Thy storm-tossed soul shall find
    Eternal rest !

1869.

"PEACE, BE STILL."

" And He said unto the sea, Peace, be still."

THE sky is wild and dark,
    The waves are high ;
Tossed is the broken bark,
    And the disciples think that death is nigh.
        Yet need they fear none ill—
            JESUS is there !
            He, answering their prayer,
        Says—" Peace, be still."

What though the sea should rave,
    And wind should wail !
His is the power to save ;
    Fear not the billows in the angry gale :
        Obedient to His will,
            Wind, wave, and sky
            Hear the commanding cry
        Of—" Peace, be still."

Life is a troubled sea;
  And, tempest-tossed,
Our souls oft fearfully
  Cry out in weak despair—" Lord, we are lost."
    But from God's holy hill,
      Through darkness wild,
      The cry, so meek and mild,
    Comes—" Peace, be still."

O words so full of power
  From gentlest Voice !
Though clouds of doubt should lower,
  We will dispel the gloom, and bid rejoice ;
    Our doubting hearts shall fill
      With joy and love,
      Hearing the Voice above
    Say—" Peace, be still ! "

1870.

"HE TURNETH THE SHADOW OF DEATH INTO THE MORNING."

WITHOUT, the world is bright and fair,
  The sunlight gleams upon it all ;
Within that darkened chamber there
  Strange shadows fall.

The eyes grow dim.   O LORD of Light !
  To Thee are stretched hands pale and thin ;
The shadows, deepening with the night,
  Still gather in.

Darker—more dark ; a night there is,
  On which the morning ne'er shall break ;
But we have hope—our plea is this :
  "For JESUS' sake."

1874.

NEW-YEAR HYMN.

[*This and the three following Hymns were written for Sabbath-school children.*]

O LORD of Light ! Eternal King !
  Who Ancient art of Days,
To Thee our songs we humbly sing :
  Oh ! hear our feeble praise.

With hope and love, with joy and fear,
  We wait Thy heavenly will ;
As in the past, in this New Year,
  Be Thou our Father still.

And o'er Life's dark and troubled tide,
  Through all its blinding foam,
Of our frail bark be Thou the Guide,
  And steer us safely home.

Some faces loved have passed away :
  Still we are gathered here,
On this Thy holy Sabbath day
  To greet the glad New Year ;—

To praise Thy name, Most Holy One !
  Thou art our trust alone :
May we, when all the years are done,
  Be gathered round Thy throne.

Accept, O Lord ! our humble song ;
  Hear us, Thou Prince of Peace !
To Thee for aye shall praise belong
  When death and time shall cease.

1873.

NEW-YEAR HYMN.

O LORD of Life! Eternal King!
  Who Ancient art of Days,
In this New Year to Thee we sing,
  Oh! hear our humble praise.

With voices soft, in accents low,
  We stand about Thy feet;
And praise Thy name, while some we know
  Have joined the mercy-seat.

Another Year! Time's ceaseless tide
  Bears many a feeble bark;
Sweet JESUS! be the children's Guide
  And Helmsman in the dark.

We cannot see, we do not know,
  We cling about Thy form;
For without Thee we cannot go
  Out in the whirling storm.

Year in, year out—in woe, in weal,
   Be with us on the way;
Give us Thy hand, that we may feel
   Thou art our Guide and Stay.

Then years may roll, and time may fly,
   Our hope is firm and strong;
Until, far up, beyond the sky,
   We sing a richer song.

1874.

NEW-YEAR HYMN.

ONCE again, O Heavenly Father!
　To Thy presence near,
We, Thy happy children, gather
　Round Thy footstool here,
　　　Still before Thee
　　　To adore Thee
　In the glad New Year.

Hear our childish voices blending
　As we sing Thy praise;
May our hymn, to heaven ascending,
　Blend with angels' lays!
　　　Voices raise we
　　　Still to praise Thee
　Through the years and days.

Unknown future lies before us;
　Is the distance dim?
JESUS still is watching o'er us;
　We will trust in Him.
　　　Sing one song, then,
　　　Maidens, young men,
　Child, and cherubim!

Glory, glory, hallelujah!
    Let our praises ring,
Father, Son, and Spirit Holy,
    We with angels sing.
        Hallelujah!
        Hallelujah!
    To our Lord and King!

1875.

NEW-YEAR HYMN.

" Glory be to GOD on High !"—
   Hear the rich angelic song
Wafted to us from the sky !
   We the echoes will prolong.

To the King a thousand years
   Are but as a single day ;
Praise and bless the God who hears
   Even the child that kneels to pray.

Thus with hope we gather here
   On the holy Sabbath days ;
And again in this New Year
   Sing we to our Father's praise.

Jesus ! we would look to Thee ;
   All the gifts we have are Thine :
" Let the children come to Me,"—
   Once was said in Palestine.

G

So, together singing here,
   Upon Thee our hope is cast ;
Guide us in the coming year ;
   Thou didst lead us through the last.

Thou hast given us health and friends,
   Youth and happiness and love ;
And Thy goodness never ends,
   Showering blessings from above.

Shall not we take up the song,
   And our voices reach the sky ?
Singing praises loud and long,—
   "GLORY BE TO GOD ON HIGH !"

1876.

Life Musings.

———◆———

BREAD.

TO toil and moil,
    Early and late,
Poor Humanity,
    This is thy fate !
Go to the town, with its noise and din,
Look at the faces pinched and thin ;
Hear the tramp of hurrying feet,
As men jostle and push on the crowded street.
Ever, for ever, they strive and strain,
Wearing and tearing nerve and brain,
Selfishly each one trying to gain,—
What ? Not money, or honour, or fame,
But a little fuel to feed the flame
Of the fire of life, which must be fed ;
And the strife is the struggle for daily Bread.

Buy or sell
　　Whatever you may ;
　　Hammer or spin
　　　Night and day.
Since man first fought with the sulky soil,
Harder and harder has grown his toil,
Till now, with the very struggle and strife
In trying to live, men wear out life.
See the mother attending the factory wheels,
Trying to stifle the love she feels,
While over her heart there gently steals
A thought of the child in her lonely cot :
Is it crying for food, which she has not got ?
Bread ! Bread ! that is the cry :
Well, work very hard, and you may not die !

Sweat of the brow,
　　Sweat of the brain—
　　These are the wages
　　　Of sin, the pain
Which fell on man when he fell from God,
And was banished from Eden's bless'd abode.
Trying to grasp intangible breath,
And drive away the fear of death,
Man labours for that *which perisheth.*

Generations of men, they come and they go,
Like the restless tide, with its ebb and flow ;
One passes for ever out of the strife,
One rises behind to fight for life ;
· And the wail of the world, as it whirls through
    space,
Ever pierces the "high and the lofty place."

1869.

CALM AND STORM.

I.

Buoyed on the tide,
We gently glide
Over the glassy sea;
And the wavelets, rippling, break on the side
Of the ship right merrily.
Sailing away,
We follow the day,
Though we know that his work is done;
Behind us rises the twilight gray,
But our goal is the setting sun.

Smooth is the sea
As sea could be,
Cloudless the evening sky;
And the sunbeam flickering up on the mast
Flirts with the pennon high.
All is so fair,
We may banish care
As we gallantly sail to the west;
When the sunlight passes before us there,
The sea will rock us to rest.

II.

Dark as the grave,
Each hollow wave
Rises up in the night;
And the night-wind, taking the sea in its arms,
Shaketh the ship in its might.
At midnight hour
Dark tempests lower,
And the storm hath broken our sail;
But the tattered rag is a fitting flag
Of the spirit that raised the gale.

Waters flushing,
Crashing, rushing,
Thunder their strength on the deck;
And the poor ship, staggering under the weight,
Drifteth, a broken wreck.
Driven and tossed,
For ever lost,
And no one there who could save,
Oh! who can tell of the horror that fell
On that ship that sunk in the wave!

1869.

A STREET SCENE.

THERE, in the blinding sleet,
　In a night so cold and wild,
Standing alone in the street,
　Singeth a little child.

His feet are red and bare,
　And the passers to and fro
Pity him standing there,
　Ankle-deep in the snow.

Young, but shrunk like the old,
　Wet in the snow and rain,
Singing his grief in the cold,
　He sobbeth away his pain.

And his face is young and fair,
　Standing out in the storm;
For under the gas-light's glare
　We see his shivering form.

Of " Home, sweet Home " he sings,
   If such a place there be ;
To his eye a tear it brings,
   For never a home has he.

No place to lay his head,
   Fatherless must he roam,
Wishing that he were dead,
   And passed through the darkness—*Home !*

1869.

"SILENCE IS GOLDEN."

FAR from the city with its ceaseless strife,
　　Here, where all things are still,
　　Within the shadow of the hill,
I thought of all the clamour of our life :

Of all the talking of poor foolish man,
　　The babbling of the crowd,
　　Which ever rises loud,
Jarring God's music since the world began.

I thought of life, with all its care and cark ;
　　Of man who ever cries,
　　As ceaselessly he tries
To grasp the truth while groping in the dark.

O man ! let thy poor mutterings pass away,
　　Let all thy janglings cease,
　　And strive for lasting peace,
And hear what golden silence has to say.

Heed not the teaching of a thousand fools,
    Who know not wrong from right,
    Who think the darkness light;
Truth is not in the cavil of the schools.

For God's own everlasting hills which stand,
    In all their giant might,
    So silent in the night,
Teach more than all the talkers in the land.

The silent stars call on us to rejoice;
    Christ brooded on the hills,
    Of life and all its ills,—
Hear, ye who may, the echo of His voice!

1869.

JEDBURGH ABBEY.

O GRAY old Ruin ! let me stand and gaze,
   In the fair twilight of this closing day,
Through all the mist of time, the hallowed haze,
   Which shrouds in gloom the ages passed away.

Wisdom is old, the outcome of the years,
   And these old stones have seen the ages die,—
Have seen men pass, with all their hopes and fears,
   Fade out, like stars before the morning sky.

Where are the men who shaped these goodly stones ?
   Where are the monks who filled the house with
      prayer ?
Through ruined aisle the night-wind, wailing, moans,
   Sobbing through broken arch—where are they?—
      where ?

Passed out of sight, " black-hooded and black stoled,"
   They went as they had come, their work was done ;
For Men and Time the Abbey bell had tolled,
   Their day had closed, a brighter age begun.

But still their temple stands, like tombstone gray,
  The silent resting-place of many years ;
And o'er the churchyard of this later day,
  The sloping shadow hides the mourner's tears.

And when we pass, the Abbey shall remain,
  For ever standing in its hallowed place,
Bearing the scourging of the wind and rain,
  The marks of time upon its aged face.

O Wind ! when passing on thy wandering way,
  Sigh through the ancient nave in twilight dim ;
And through the aisles, so very old and gray,
  Pass like the echo of a monkish hymn.

O wasting Time ! send not thy blighting blast ;
  Thy hand must gently touch this sacred spot :
For 'tis thine own, a memory of the past,
  A lasting monument of ancient thought.

O gentle Night ! as thy dark curtain falls,
  Blessing, I leave the place I love so well :
May this old ruined tower, these broken walls,
  In ages yet to come, their story tell !

1869.

BY AND BY!

By and by !
By and by !
With a heigh-ho and a long-drawn sigh,
The child is thinking of By and by !
  Sitting and gazing into the fire,
   He watches the flickering flame leap higher,
   And he sees the falling spark expire ;
And he longs, and he thinks, and he heaves his sigh,
  And he dreams of the golden By and by !

By and by !
By and by !
The road is steep, but the aim is high,
And the man is working for By and by !
  Struggling and fighting night and day,
  Selling God's time as best he may,
  He grasps at the world as it passes away ;
And he fights, and he strives, but he breathes no sigh :
  He gathers the treasure for By and by !

By and by !
By and by !
Weary and worn, with a helpless cry,
The old man waits on the By and by !
His eye is dim, and the sun is cold,
And the man is withered, and pale, and old ;
His By and by 's under the churchyard mould :
And he waits, and he longs, for his time is nigh,
And the weary shall rest in the By and by !

1869.

1 8 6 9.

HERE in my chair before the fire,
  Within the shadows of the room,
  Here sit I watching in the gloom,
To see a year expire.
  And as I sit and think,
  The wind comes sobbing through the window-
      chink,
    And from beneath the door,
      With voice which seems to cry,
      "What though the year should die,
    As other years have died before?"

There, standing on the mantel-shelf,
  The timepiece in its marble case,
  With solemn voice and sober face,
Is ticking to itself.
  Each tick, like long-drawn sigh,
  Seems ever saying that the year must die;
    And it is only right,
      That, with the passing day,
      The year should slip away,
    Like a prowling thief in the night.

O good old Year ! with many fears,
   Here must I sit and watch at last
   Thy old face vanish in the past,
And join the bygone years.
   I hear the midnight bell
  Is slowly ringing out thy funeral knell ;
    I hear the wind's weird sigh
     Sob through the leafless trees ;
     Without, the wintry breeze
    Wails feebly like a baby's cry.

H

THE MERMAIDS.

UNDER the sea !
Under the sea !
What glory is hidden
Under the sea !
'Neath the restless tide,
'Neath the surface foam,
The mermaids hide
In their coral home ;
And the green light gleams
Through the gentle wave ;
And it glimmers
And shimmers
Down into the cave,
On the beautiful things
Where the seaweed clings ;—
On the pearls and coral
And silver shells,
As they shine in the home
Where the mermaid dwells.

Under the sea !
Under the sea !
What beauty is hidden
Under the sea !
Down out of our sight,
In the light so dim,
All day and night
Do the mermaids swim ;
And the moonlight shines
On their golden hair ;
And it shivers
And quivers
As it shows how fair
Are the arms which wave
In their hidden cave ;
And a joy comes ringing
Up, merrily, free,
From the home of the mermaid
Down under the sea !

Under the sea !
Under the sea !
How strange that any
Could doubt there be
Such a lovely place
Down under the sea !—

A home of grace,
   And of joy and glee.
But still it is there,
And the mermaids fair
    In their playing
    Are saying—
" Why, we do not care,
    For man only dies
    If ever he tries
To sport in our home
   So fair and so free ;
In the home of the mermaids,
   Down under the sea !"

1870.

THE JEWEL.

Upon a bosom fair
　　A jewel gleamed ;
　And as it rose and fell,
　　With the soft swell
　　　Of Love,
　　　It seemed
Like some fair dew-drop on a rose,
　　Which, with its crown
　　　Of beauty,
　　　Bendeth down,
　When the wind blows.

" O Jewel ! rich and rare,
　　Why gleamest thou
　So coldly on the throng
　　Where mirth and song
　　　Hold now
High carnival ?   Thy place of rest
　　Should warm thy beams ;
　　　Fairer
　Should be thy gleams
From such a breast."

    " The youth and bloom shall fade,
       The laughter die,
     The joy shall pass away,
      With sadness day
        Shall come ;
         And I
Shall gleam when all the joy is dead.
      What are the years
         To me ?
       Laughter or tears
      My gleams I shed."

1870.

ALONE.

ALONE I wandered by the surging sea,
  And unto me
In darkness drear the rising tide made moan :
 Each wave seemed wailing to the silent stars,
 Each billow broke upon the sandy bars,
  And cried with grief and groan—
   Cried unto me
   In sympathy—
   " Thou art alone !"

Alone, upon the city's crowded street,
  Where hurrying feet
Tread all day long, O man, thou art alone !
 What is the whirling of the wheels to thee ?—
 A melancholy moan, which seems to be
  Crying in wearied tone,
   Through all this crowd
   Which clamours loud,
   " Thou art alone !"

Alone, even 'neath the gas-light in the rooms,
   Where sweet perfumes
Waft on the air, when youth, and joy, and love,
 And mirth, and music, mingle soul with soul ;
 When hand is clasped in hand, and o'er the
   bowl
  Friendship is pledged, a stone
    Is at the heart :—
    This poisoned dart,
   Thou art alone !

Alone, when tossing on the bed of pain,
   Love tries in vain
To ease thy couch, to smooth thy pillow down ;
 With falling tears friends gently press thy hand,
 For thee alone has come the dread command.
  Through portals wide the throne
    Gleams on thy sight :
    In death's dark night—
   Art thou alone ?

1870.

TWO HARVESTS.

[Written during the Franco-German War.]

I.

THERE is a music in the air,
    Soft and sweet—
It comes from vale and hill,
Dwells everywhere,
    Rising like incense meet,
As if our land was still
An Eden fresh and fair.
The sunlight shines upon the sheaves,
    The sickle glitters in the ripened wheat,
The swallows twitter in the eaves,
    Flowers nestle at our feet ;
The fields are white unto the harvest now,
And sloping up the mountain's brow
    Waveth the golden grain ;
    Then, gather in,
Till corn and wine abound,
    Till harvest comes again,
Till joy the year hath crowned.

II.

A cry comes from over the sea,
    Weird and wild,
Borne o'er the surging wave—
What can it be?
    It is the harvest, child—
The harvest of the grave;
The harvest reaped by thee,
O Death!   The air is full of moans,
    The trampled corn with blood of men is wet,
The quivering sky is pierced with shrieks and
        groans,
    And angry foes have met,
And ranks of men are mowed like ripened wheat,
And fall to lie beneath the feet
    Of those who reap.   The wail,
      Of bride or wife
    Comes, like the harvest song,
      Rising o'er all the strife—
    " How long? O Lord! how long?"

1870.

FRANCE.

[*Written after the German Victories in 1870.*]

LAUGHTER-LOVING, joyous France
Tripped it lightly in the dance,
Mirth and madness in her glance.

North and South, and East and West,
Came for pleasure or for rest—
Many a worn and weary guest.

And she laughed their cares away :
Mirth and music, night and day,
Taught the saddest to be gay.

Brought her handmaid, Art, to place
A new glory and a grace
Round the beauty of her face.

But the joy of France is past ;
Tears for laughter come at last—
All her sky is overcast.

Mirth and music, they are o'er ;
All the joy she showed before
Vanished now for evermore.

For the face that once was fair
Now is wrinkled o'er with care—
Ashy-white with mild despair.

And her hair, dishevelled, torn,
On the wanton breeze is borne.
Broken-hearted and forlorn,

She who danced the livelong day,
She who sang the hours away,
Humbly kneeling, tries to pray :—

" Lord, Thou knowest right from wrong,
Suffer not, nor tarry long :
Is the battle to the Strong ?"

1870.

THE OLD YEAR

1870.

OUT of the struggle of life,
  With its troubles, and sorrows, and joys,
Slipping away from the strife,
  Deafened with clamour and noise,
    Moveth the Year,
    With trembling and fear,
  Bearing his burden of care ;
    And the wild waves rave,
    As he moves to his grave :
His load it is heavy to bear.

Plodding along on his way,
  He murmurs not, neither will speak ;
He is weary, and old, and gray,
  The wild winds buffet his cheek.
    Knowing the road,
    He beareth his load,
  And over his head in the skies
    The elements crowd,
    And they weave him a shroud
To cover him up when he dies.

Bearing his burden of woe,
  He will vanish away in the night;
Cover him up in the snow,
  Huddle him out of our sight:
    Hear ye his dole,
    'Tis the battle's roll!
  With the Year may the bloodshed cease;
    Let the New one come;
    He shall silence the drum;
  For he bears the sweet olive of Peace.

THE SONG OF THE REDS.

[*Written at the time of the Commune in Paris, May, 1871.*]

We are free !
We are free !
We are free as the wind, as the fetterless wind,
The wild mad wind, which doth howl
Like a ghoul ;
Which can blow as it lists, and is strong ;
Which can fell at a stroke
The gnarled old oak
That the forest hath cherished long.

We are free
As the sea ;
As the moon-struck sea, as the pitiless sea,
When its rolling breakers roar
On the shore ;
Which can break what it likes in its joy ;
For the mightiest ship
Is but a chip
To be crushed like a baby's toy.

We are free !
Float the flag—
Republican red—kick the crown in the mud.
Here's a cap for the head,
Bloody red.
The white banner of Peace be it stained
'Neath the filth of the street,
Under trampling of feet,
For with bloodshed is liberty gained.

We were free
Once before !—
When the good guillotine poured its blood on the street,
When Reason was crowned by the crowd,
Shouting loud,
Vanished law both of God and of man :
And the people were free
Who bowed the knee
To a deified courtesan.

They were free ;
So are we,
As the wind and the sea !   Who can fetter our reign ?
Float the flag which is red
Overhead,

For our might is the sword and the flame ;
We have leave now to shoot,
This is freedom to boot,
And we'll do it in Liberty's name !

1871.

THE OWL.

TEE whit, tee whoo!
Cries the owl from the belfry tower;
'Tis midnight, and the hour
    Comes throbbing from the bell;
The watchful owl, whose words are strange and few,
Replies—Tee whit, tee who-o-o!

The fair moon gleams
Upon the graves, and throws its light
Upon the headstones white,
    Which cluster round the church;
And on the tower, where climbs the ivy green,
.It throws a silver sheen.

The sombre yew
Rustles and shivers in the breeze
Which sigheth through the trees,
    And like a spirit moves;
The hamlet sleeps: sadly the stillness through
Comes this—Tee whit, tee who-o-o!

Tee whit, tee whoo!
The owl which on the belfry sits,
Where now the black bat flits,
   Will cry, when those who sleep
In village hushed, are laid beneath the yew,
This cry—Tee whit, tee who-o-o!

1871.

THE YOUNG SAMARITAN.

[An incident of the neglected Children's free dinners in Edinburgh.]

CAULD's the wind that blaws sae wearie
    Through the closes o' the toon,
An' it soughs an' sabs sae eerie,
    As the blast comes blatterin' doon ;
Rain an' sleet are baith unitin'
    At the corners wi' a swirl ;
An' the cauld's sae keenly bitin'
    That our fingers fairly dirl.

See that wee bit shilpit callant,
    Wi' the laddie on his back !
Where's he gaun ?   He's geyan wullant,
    Dirt and duds he doesna lack.
He is carryin' the wee ane,
    For he canna gang his lane ;
Gaun to get his dinner gied him,
    For at hame he wad get nane.

Has he faither? Has he mother?
  If he has, what can they be?
Is the wee ane, then, his brother?
  Faith, he kens na wha is he :
But he carries him fu' gently,
  An' he sees him get his share.
" There's a laddie, noo ! tak tent ye ! "
  An' his hame—a common stair !

1871.

.

UNDERTONE.

THROUGH the old cathedral swelling
     Music floats ;
Through the ancient nave are welling
     Organ notes ;
Through the aisle, so old and dim,
Comes the holy evening hymn ;
And the voices of the choir,
     As they rise
To the groinèd roof, expire.
Song like that of Paradise,
Surely truest praise is this :
    Gloria in excelsis !

Music dieth, but its soul,
     Undertone,
Floats immortal to its goal,
     Heaven's throne,
Through the still and silent night,
To the realms of joy and light.
As our heart-throb beats the time,

Wells our praise;
And our spirits' song doth chime
With the angels' holy lays,
As they chant in realms of bliss,
Where the home of music is.

1871.

SIR WALTER SCOTT:

A Centenary Ode.

Here will we rest us in this hazel wood,
  Within the shadow of the leafy trees ;
To muse awhile alone in thoughtful mood,
  Lulled by the murmur of the summer breeze.
The shallow streamlet rippling at our feet
  Maketh sweet music, babbling soft and low,
The fluttering leaves reply in accents meet,
While song-birds' throbbing notes in thrilling trebles
    flow.

Far from the city, with its toil and strife,
  And noise of trampling feet, and dust, and din ;
Its streets and crescents, with their pride of life,
  Its lanes and alleys, with their vice and sin ;
Here, far from these, we view the purple hills,—
  Old Scotland's hills, by Scotsmen ne'er forgot :
One look of these with pride the patriot fills ;—
He thinks of Wallace, Bruce, of Burns, and Walter Scott.

And is it, then, a hundred years since he,
  The latest, gentlest minstrel of the North,
Did clap his little hands in childish glee
  At a great thunderstorm, when, belching forth,
The livid lightning wrapped the hills in flame?
  Crowing and kicking in his Scottish plaid,
Lay "Wattie Scott," till those who left him came,
And found, all safe and sound, the babe where he'd
    been laid.

There was a wizard once, both weird and old,
  Whose magic charms could split the hills in three;
Of whom in bated breath strange tales were told:
  Another Wizard rose, more great than he!
We speak of him with love; his powerful wand
  Touched hill, lake, river, glen, and barren scaur;
It blazed a glory on our native land
Which spread its fame and his to countries near and far.

O SCOTT! with thy enchanting wand,—the pen,
  Well couldst thou conjure spirits strange and rare;
The ruined castle clangs with armèd men;
  In broken bower we find the lady fair;
In lonely glen resounds the staghound's bay;
  In ancient hall still harps the minstrel old;
Or through some ruined nave of abbey gray,
We hear the monks' sad chant of "*Dies iræ*" rolled!

But not to scenes like these he led alone,—
    Times past and present were alike portrayed;
He shows us " fickle Bess " upon her throne,
    And then in colours true a beggar maid :
He knew our little life with all its fears,
    Its laughter, sadness, joy, its good and ill;
His page inspired anon draws silent tears,
Or with true mirth and joy does saddest bosom fill.

We've followed where he led to strangest scenes,
    Some grave, some sad, some tender, many gay :
We've been at Muschat's Cairn with Jeanie Deans,
    Or caught with Cuddie Headrigg " scaldin' broo !"
We've seen sweet Amy Robsart's fatal fall;
    Or heard Brown knocking at Rough Dandie's door;
" Doon, Mustard, doon,"—we hear the farmer call :
Then comes mad Norna's chant when northern tempests
      roar.

Auld Edie Ochiltree, we know him well,
    So rich in wit, in gear however poor ;
Adown our cheek the silent tear-drop fell
    For yon sweet, ill-starred "Bride of Lammermoor."
The Dominie croaks loud " pro-di-gi-ous !"
    Then comes a lullaby, sweet, soft, and low ;
We hear old Bailie Jarvie's frightened fuss ;
Romance immortal lives preserved in " Ivanhoe."

Those household names Scott's mighty power may
    prove,
  And men unborn shall cherish still his name;
As long as time shall last, or woman love,
    Succeeding ages shall increase his fame.
The book lives long although the author dies,—
    Lives to be loved by peoples yet to be;
Though Walter Scott in Dryburgh Abbey lies,
His name is still kept fresh by "Old Mortality."

O gray old Scotland! rocky, barren, wild,
    For thee has warrior borne the battle's brunt;
For thee, "meet nurse," has sung poetic child:
    Long mayest thou proudly rear thy craggy front!
Long may thy hardy sons, both near and far,
    Still love the land which ne'er can be forgot;
More rich than pampas wild is barren scaur,
For Scotland, old and gray, is still the land of Scott!

1871.

"WHAT MIGHT HAVE BEEN."

I READ me a poem not long ago,
  'Twas in June, when the woods were green ;—
A poem dejected, and sad, and low,
  By one who, in sorrow keen,
Sobbed out through his verses' rhythmical flow,
  And sighed for " what might have been."

He sang of the past in a wearied tone,
  And his song my sympathies led :
I thought of the past, and made my moan
  For a joy which had vanished and fled ;
'Neath the leaves of the forest I stood alone,
  And longed for a love which was dead.

But the sun burst out in his pride of noon,
  And the birds sang sweet on the spray ;
And my heart rose up in its strength, and soon
  I thought of a happier day.
" Let the love-sick maiden beneath the moon
  Sigh for love which has passed away."

"What might have been!"—'Tis another song
   The poet must sing to me;
The past is past; its memories throng
   In our hearts, but still we are free;
And the singer should sing full rich and strong
   Of the happiness *yet to be.*

"What might have been"—is a vain regret;
   "What may be,"—a purpose high:
Though sorrow and tears in our life have met,
   Oh! why should we listlessly sigh?
The future may hold some happiness yet;
   It is better to do than to die.

Ye singers who hold life's music sweet,
   Oh! why need ye cling to its tears?
Sing us songs of joy, and our hearts will beat
   With hope, while we banish our fears.
Sing loud and full, in a language meet,
   Of the joy of the golden years.

1871.

THE MEETING.

[An incident not noticed in " Leaves from the Journal of our Life in the Highlands."]

I.

FAR from the town with its noise and stir,
    Where all is still
On the Highland moors, but the plover's whirr
    And the bleating of sheep on the hill;

Slowly along by the mountain-side, very slow,
    On the lonely road,
Moves a humble cart; and, behind it, stooping low,
    Cometh the man who mourns for its load.

He, and his sons, and some friends who can feel;
    This is it all;—
Only his wife in a coffin of deal,
    Laid upon straw, and no funeral pall

II.

Away from the Castle gates, joyous they whirl
        Through uplands green ;
By the turn of the hill where the dust-clouds swirl,—
      Light-hearted and happy, the Prince and the
        Queen !

" Stop ! What is this that is coming near ?
        Draw to a side : "—
" It is only a poor woman's humble bier,
      And a poor man trying his grief to hide."

Slowly they passed, and there the Prince upstood,
        Head bent, and bare ;
The peasant's grief the royal rank subdued :
      God of one blood hath made His children share !

1873.

THE NIGHT-LAMP.

BURNING dimly every night
　　In a chamber-window high,
　　In a window next the sky,
Flickers aye a feeble light,
　　Gleams and shimmers when the roar
　　And the whirl of traffic's o'er ;
　　When the cold deserted street
　　Only echoes to the tramp
Of the watchman on his beat.

When the night is dark and chill,
　　And the slanting scourging rain
　　Beats and blatters on the pane,
There the light is burning still.
　　When the moon is shining bright
　　Every hour of every night,
　　Much more constant than the moon,
　　Or the multitude of stars,
Burns the lamp there late and soon.

Do you wonder what's the light
    In that chamber-window high—
    Glimmering up against the sky,
Burning dimly every night?
    'Tis a woman watching only
    By a sick-bed, sad and lonely,
Watching patiently and well—
    Oh how gently, and how sweetly !
Oh how fondly ! none can tell. .

1874.

HOLIDAY.

WEARILY every day
 Grinding away,
Plodding and planning for ever and aye ;
Scheming by night and working by day,
In the noisy town with its smoke and din,
Trying to gather the treasure in,
Our faces grow haggard, and pinched, and thin :
Then Hurrah ! Hurrah ! for our holiday !
To mountain and moor we are off and away,
That the languid limbs and the wearied brain
In the breath of the heather new vigour may gain.

Joyously, happily,
 Climbing the hill,
We move no more like the horse in the mill.
Tramping the heath, and leaping the rill,
Breathing the mountain air, fragrant and sweet,
Crossing the bog and fen, treading the peat,
Frighting the plover that whirrs from our feet ;
Then Hurrah ! Hurrah ! we will climb if we can
The brows of the giant Ben Cruachan ;
With our sparkling eyes, and our faces brown,
We are far enough now from the noisy town.

Happily, merrily,
Carelessly free,
Now at the farmer's board laughing with glee,
Laughing and chaffing, most happy are we ;
Then in the little kirk over the moor,
Quietly, seriously, looking demure,
Wondering at worship so simple and pure.
List to the bell in the morning air
Sweetly tinkling its call to prayer !
See how the cloud-shadows float on the hill :
The breeze seems to whisper the woods to be still.

Back again willingly,
Holidays o'er,
To the town, where for ever, with echo and roar,
Flows the tide of Life on its stony shore.
Pushing and jostling and scrambling, still
Amongst men we must work, and we'll work with a will
All the better for breathing the air of the hill.
When we rest we can dream of the glorious Ben,
Of lake and of mountain, of moorland and glen,
Of our laughter light, and the farmer's cheer,
And the tinkling bell, which the worshippers hear.

1874.

INCHKEITH.

BEHIND me there the old town rears
    Its jagged front to clouded skies,
        And nestling sweet,
        By Arthur's Seat,
    Gray Holyrood in shadow lies ;
        While over there,
        On street and square,
    On monument and tower and spire,
        The red sun beams,
        In setting gleams,
    And all the Forth's aglow with fire.

The river glints in gold and green,
    And emerald islands gem the wave ;
        When fails the light,
        And silent night
    Shall throw o'er all its mantle grave,
        Then o'er the sea
        Right faithfully
    The lighthouse sheds its helpful ray ;

On heaving tides
Its glimmer glides,
To cheer the sailor on his way.

Though now the glittering waters lave,
And laugh and ripple round the rock,
Maybe ere night,
In giant might,
The storm will come with thunder shock;
The angry wave
Will leap and rave :
But darkness can't this light eclipse—
It still must shine,
A lamp divine,
A beacon-fire for drifting ships.

Year in, year out, it still revolves,
We watch it come and disappear;
Like those who sail,
We gladly hail
The light by which the helmsmen steer.
It ceaseless turns,
Still steady burns,
Alternating the dark and light ;
The glorious stream
Shall ever gleam,
And circle through the wildest night.

Ah ! many an eager eye has gazed
    From rocking deck when night was still,
        If through the dark
        Would gleam the spark
    Which now I'm watching from the hill.
        Long may the light
        Shine clear and bright,
    A joy it is by shore or sea :
        The sailor's bride
        Looks o'er the tide ;
    The landsman greets it from the lea.

1875.

BACK TO THE HAMLET.

WITH his mother's blessing,
And his sister's caressing,
He went away from the hamlet still,
Into the city for good or for ill.

Ah! what a pity!
The surging city
Drew him into its eddying stream!
He struggled, and fought, and dreamed his dream.

And this is the ending:
Slowly wending
(This is the ending now of it all)
Back again to the hamlet small—

Into the churchyard:
Here not a sound is heard
But the lark's sweet song in the summer sky,
And the grass is green, and the graves are high.

1875.

TELEGRAPH WIRES.

OVER the land for miles,
By hamlet, village, and town,
By the glebe where the landscape smiles,
By flowery meadow and down,
Skirting the edge of the lake,
List to the music I make ;
For the zephyr still sings
Through my tremulous strings
As my wonderful journey I take.

Over the hedgerows white,
Under the hawthorn's spray,
I glitter and flash in the light
Which glints through the trees on my way.
Beeches and elms and limes,
Where the ivy plant clingeth and climbs ;
And down at my feet,
Nestling tender and sweet,
The wild flowers blossom by times.

Along by the road so still,
  Over the mountain's ridge,
Reaching from valley to hill,
  Booming up there on the bridge,
In the night at the cross-roads lone,
In the wind do I groan and moan;
    By the old churchyard
    Is the sound still heard
Of the telegraph's monotone.

Up by the railway track,
  Still long drawn-out and fine,
Where the echoes are thundering back,
  As the engine comes down the line,
I hum,—an Æolian lyre;
But the monster, with heart of fire
    And iron bones,
    Ne'er heedeth the tones
Of the miles and miles of wire.

Under the depths of the deep,
  Hidden from sun and sky,
There where the sleepers sleep
  Till the Day which is drawing nigh;

Under the storm and swell,
Tangled with sea-weed and shell,
    By the riven decks
    Of the sunken wrecks,
And treasures no tongue can tell.

North, South, and West, and East,
   Then over the roofs of the town—
Here has the journey ceased,
   Where the lines come lowering down.
'Neath the ocean, or over the land,
Who has them all at command?
    Flashing the fire
    O'er the miles of wire,
Is a girl with the tiniest hand.

1876.

FLOWERS IMMORTAL.

Poets oft in song or lyric
 Sing that flowers are transient things ;
"See them fade !"—says dull empiric,
 Echoing what the poet sings.
  Kingdoms, empires—waxing, waning ;
  Flowers with us are still remaining,
 Stronger than the works of kings.

Streaming from its eastern portal,
 When the sun first lit the skies,
Frailest flowers, with love immortal,
 Heavenward turned their longing eyes,
  Where, within the long-lost Aiden,
  Mother Eve, like any maiden,
 Roses plucked in Paradise.

And to-day, in endless reaches,
 Where the streamlet murmurs low,
Underneath the shady beeches,
 Still the wild flowers bloom and blow—
  Daisies, bluebells, daffodillies ;
  And the lesson of the lilies
 Is the same as long ago.

And for us, when time has ended,
　　In the dark and silent tomb,
Violets and daisies, blended,
　　Over us may sweetly bloom.
　　　History repeats its story :
　　　Primroses will have their glory,
　　Mignonette its rich perfume.

1876.

IN THE PORCH.

WHAT does she on the street?
Rain-drops they patter and beat,
Rain and the pitiless sleet
    Cruelly pelt her;
Slips she now into the porch,
Into the porch of the church,
Where she is stamping her feet,
    Seeking for shelter.

Only a girl very fair,
Laughing now, what does she care?
Hearing the voice of the prayer,
    Casting from off her
The glittering drops of the rain,
Thinks she the prayer is in vain?
Backward now shaking her hair,
    Is she a scoffer?

Voices of children now raise
Heavenward sweetly their praise;
Listening—how changed is her gaze!
    Looking and longing:

Now are the flashing eyes dim ;
Thoughts have been stirred by the hymn,—
Thoughts of her innocent days,
　　Memories thronging.

Still is the street dark and wet,
The sleet and the wind they have met ;
In the porch, with her features hard set,
　　Will she not stay?
Once could she sing with the band
Of the fair and the far " Happy Land ; "
Her heart it is echoing yet,—
　　" Far away ! "

1876.

A NATIONAL CHARACTERISTIC.

" It is part of the old Scottish severe unsparing character—
cold to calmness outside—tender to agony, burning to fierceness
within."—BROWN'S " *Horæ Subsecivæ.*"

You say we Scotch are stolid, cold—
　　An unimpressionable race ;
Before you came you had been told,
　　If they feel aught, you cannot trace
Their joy or grief, for young or old
　　Will show no sign upon the face.

You think our hearts are hard as steel,
　　Because to all we do not show
The joy and sorrow that we feel
　　In laughter loud, or moaning woe.
Against your statement I appeal :
　　'Tis only that you do not know.

" I love you well,"—an artist said,
　　Last season as the autumn fell,
To one who, hidden in her plaid,
　　Thrilled as he vowed he loved her well.
" Can you return my love, sweet maid ? "—
　　The Scottish lassie would not tell.

There in that cottage up the hill,
  With gentle smile and pallid brow,
The girl is dying, thinking still,—
  Ah ! no one knows he broke his vow !
Her heart was his for good or ill,
  And it is breaking for him now.

Perhaps if you will wait a week,
  Her father there will lay her low :
No tear will fall upon his cheek,
  No hint of grief, no sign of woe.
Sorrow is sacred ; he will speak
  No more of her who lies below.

The shallow streamlet makes the noise ;
  How silent flows the river deep !
The tear-dimmed eye, the broken voice,
  Tell others what we fain would keep.
We cannot talk about our joys ;
  Our hearts will break before we weep.

1876.

THE SILENT MONITOR.

[*Over the gate of the Cemetery of Brechin is carved the face of a woman, with a finger laid upon the lips, and no motto affixed.*]

WHAT meaneth this face
    So still and so lone,
Which looks down from its place
With womanly grace,
      And, though silent, still seemeth to moan?
        One finger's tip
        Is placed on its lip :
Come, read me this riddle in stone.

We will stand and wait
    To know the command
Which, early and late,
This face o'er the gate
      Gives to all with its stony hand :—
        "Drop ye the tear,
        But speak not here,
For within is the Silent Land !"

'Tis the Cemetery old
    Where the cypress waves :
Hither brought to the mould
Have been faces as cold
    As the face which so patiently braves
        The wind and rain,
        Which sayeth again,—
    " Keep silence !"—"Tread softly on graves !"

1876.

THE CAGED LARK.

LOVELY is the morning,
  And the river looks like glass ;
Diamonds of dew-drops
  Glint and glitter on the grass ;
While the golden sunlight beams
  On the fields so fresh and fair ;
And it glances on the streams,
And it flashes, and it gleams
      Everywhere.

And above the ploughman
  As he plods with heavy feet,
The lark in heaven cloudless
  Sings its matins clear and sweet.
'Tis so happy to be free ;
  All the sky is its estate ;
Springing upward from the lea,
Singing where you cannot see,
      At heaven's gate.

And here, below a window,
   From a cage with iron bars,
Comes a gush of melody ;
   Oh ! how its sweetness jars
On our ear ! It is not meet
   That the silence should be broke
With a song so clear and sweet
In the dry and dusty street,
      Among the smoke.

1877.

THE WEDDING DRESS.

An hour or two we had been wed,
    I'm sure it was not any more,
When flowers were showered upon your head,
As through the hall with me you fled,
    And crossed the threshold of the door.

And glad we were to get away
    From all the talking and the noise,
The babble and the laughter gay,
The happy bustle of the day
    When first we tasted nuptial joys.

Back in the carriage neither spoke,
    So pleased we were to leave the press,
Till, with my arms about your cloak,
I was the first who silence broke,
    With—" Darling, where's your marriage
        dress ?"

And you leant back with feigned surprise—
   " White dresses are for maiden life ; "
With folded palms, most wondrous wise,
You said, with love-light in your eyes,—
   " And not for lawful wedded wife."

'Twas left behind you at " The Grange ; "
   Of maidenhood you had enough :
And surely 'twas not very strange
That with the life the dress should change,
    And wives should wear a homelier stuff.

But while I take this for my theme,
   You must not think that you are meant ;
From maid to matron !—well, I deem
The change of life is too extreme,
    In banishment of sentiment.

The maiden, erewhile fancy free,
   Is fond of blossoms in her hair :
She loves the stars, the moon, the sea,
The wild flowers blooming on the lea ;
    To her the world is bright and fair.

Full well to please she knows the art,
    At ball, and rout, and game, and play ;
She loves the songs that thrill the heart,
Beethoven, Mendelssohn, Mozart :
    Thus passes maidenhood away.

Life's tune is played on other strings ;
    How great the change who can express ?
The matron very seldom sings,
Her heart is full of other things ;—
    She has put off her wedding dress.

Ah ! household cares fill up the year !
    You know a music sweeter yet
Than any sound to mother's ear ;
How fast you run whene'er you hear
    Our baby in the bassinet.

1877.

THE PANTOMIME CHILD.

I KNOW your heart with pity beats,
    You know that cold and hunger kill;
The misery that one sometimes meets
Even in the fashionable streets
    Is fit enough to make one ill.

Perhaps you've often heard it said
    One half the world cannot show
How the other half doth get its bread;
Or where it lives, or how it's fed,
    They neither know, nor care to know.

You, Lady, would not set your foot
    One step adown the dirty lane :
With gathered dress and dainty boot,
Your rich attire would never suit;
    And then the sights would give you pain.

I know your heart is tender, good;
    I know you'll pity while I tell
My story: yet I think you would
Perhaps consider I was rude
    If that same lane I pictured well.

Of thieves and worse than thieves the haunt,
    The dirty, drunken, wretched, cruel;
Here must they sin, or suffer want,
For honesty brings hunger gaunt,—
    A strange reversal of the rule.

Poor, shivering, hungry, starved with cold,
    I saw a little girlie there,
With eyes of blue, and hair like gold;
Her age was six, she frankly told,
    Her little feet were red and bare.

Perhaps you'll scarcely think it true,
    But I could not forget the face:
I know that you have seen her too,
You kindly praised her eyes of blue;—
    'Twas in a very different place.

Do you remember yesternight,
 When laughing at the Pantomime,
'Mid noise of music, blaze of light,
When all around was warm and bright,
 And children marched in measured time?

And you went home to light and heat,
 And love and happiness, the while
The blue-eyed girl upon the street,
With slush and snow about her feet,
 At midnight sought her quarters vile.

1877.

NEW-YEAR'S EVE.

NIGHT is the time for rest and sleep,
When silence and darkness, calm and deep,
  Brood over valley and hill;
When the tremulous stars their vigils keep,
  When the city is hushed and still:
    To-night we must watch and wait;
Without there's a noise of hurrying feet,
And a whirl of wheels on the stony street,
    Though the night is dark and late.

It is not now as it was of old;
"Work while it is day"—we were told,
  "No man can work in the night:"
In the struggle for knowledge, or pleasure, or gold,
  The day is too short for the fight;—
    List to the factory's din,
The student is burning the midnight oil,
Nor day, nor night, is there end to our toil,
    As the gear we gather in.

All through the night to their music sweet,
The revellers dance with regular beat,
  'Mid laughter, and love, and flowers;

They turn and twirl with their flying feet,
 As they merrily chase the hours.
  Up there in a chamber dim,
A woman is soothing a loved one's pains :
While the gambler yonder pockets his gains ;
  The wine-cup is filled to the brim.

But why does the maiden so sweet and fair
Stop in the dance, with finger in air ?
  The student turn from his book ?
And the sick-nurse rise from her watching chair
  With an eager and anxious look ?
   The workman stops : Does the gambler fear ?
While he who holdeth the brimming cup,
Pauses half-way as he lifts it up,
  The stroke of the clock to hear.

Clashing aloft from turret and tower,
Tinkled with music, thundered with power,
  'Tis thus that the Year must expire :
The bells are proclaiming the midnight hour
  From belfry, and steeple, and spire ;
   While we listen with hope and fear.
Is it for this that they silently wait ?—
The round of the clock is the wheel of fate ;
  'Tis the Death and Birth of a Year.

 1877.

THOUGHTS OF HOME.

I WAS walking home in the evening ;
   And quickly I hurried on,
Through the streets of a foreign city,
   A stranger, and alone.

My thoughts to the past went backward ;
   And sadly I thought of the day
When I left the home of my childhood,
   In the old world—far away.

I thought of my weeping mother,
   As she kissed me at the door ;
I remember the blessing my father gave
   When parting on the shore.

And while thus I plodded, dreaming
　　Of home that winter night,
Right on the side-walk streaming,
　　Gleamed a brilliant ray of light.

I thought some kindly angel
　　Had let this cheering ray
Slip through some chink of Heaven
　　To light me on my way.

I looked through a blindless window,
　　And there I saw the light,
Which lifted away the sorrow,
　　And cheered my heart that night.

A lamp shone bright on a table,
　　Amid happy faces around,
And the faces were fair and lovely,
　　Where no trace of sorrow was found.

There sat a father and mother,
　　And listened while there sung
And played, one of their daughters,
　　Who looked so happy and young.

And I also stood and listened
  To the music of her song,
And a prayer went up from the darkness—
  "God keep them happy long!"

But the blind was drawn, and passing,
  I went again on my way;
And the light, I thought, was an angel's light,
  Which spoke of a happier day.

1869.

HEARTS AND HANDS.

THE sky is clear and cloudless,
　And the earth is very fair,
And our hearts are filled with gladness,
　There is music in the air ;
For the marriage-bells are ringing,
　　　Hearts and hands !
In the gray old turret swinging,
Their iron tongues are singing—
　　　Hearts and hands !
　　　Hearts and hands !
And the bride, with flowers and blushes,
　Trembling, at the altar stands—
Trembling at the joy which rushes
　At the clasping of the hands,
　　　Hearts and hands !
And the ring, the glistening token,
　Seals the joy the bells have spoken—
Binds together youth and beauty,
　　　Hearts and hands !

Making love the strongest duty.
Life may run in golden sands,
But you never
Can dissever
Those so bound with loving bands—
Bound together
Now for ever,
Hearts and hands !
Loving hearts and youthful hands.

1869.

M

L I L Y.

LILY, with the laughing eyes,
　　Babbles nonsense all the day;
Runs, and trips, and laughs, and cries,
　　Making all the noise she may.
But when falls the twilight gray,
　　When the daylight leaves the skies,
Then her laughter dies away,
　　All her merriment and glee,
All her mirth-provoking ways;—
　　Kneeling at her mother's knee,
　　　　Lily prays.

In her gown as white as snow,
　　Whispering prayer in language meet,
With her fair head bending low,
　　Kneeling at her mother's feet,

Lisps she words in accent sweet;
　Angels hovering to and fro
Bear them to the mercy-seat,—
　Bear them to the golden throne;
Seraphs hush their heavenly lays,
　Listening to the childish tone;—
　　Lily prays.

1869.

FORSAKEN.

WHEN will the wind cease sighing,
　　Sobbing and crying?
　　The leaves on the trees
　　　Are blown about
　　　With the breeze,
　　And the light of my life
　　　Has gone out.
Oh! when will he come, my dearie?
The wind blows wild and dreary,
And I am weary, weary.

When will my heart cease longing?
　　Memories thronging
　　Come out from the past.
　　　I am alone,
　　　And the blast
　　Of the north, with its cry
　　　And its moan,
Says—"When will he come, my dearie?"
The wind is cold and dreary,
And I am weary, weary.

1869.

LUCILLE.

Lucille was fair,
Lucille was sad,
As she stood on her balconie ;
Lucille she sighed, and she almost cried,
For her lover she watched to see.
And her eyes grew dim
As she sighed for him—
"Oh ! when will he come to me ?"

Mentone was brave,
And Mentone was gay,
As he sailed o'er the moon-lit wave ;
His oars they dip, and with jewels drip,
Where the glittering waters lave ;
And his voice it rings,
For joy he sings :
His lady he sails to save.

Lucille she gazed,
And her head she raised,
And she said,—" He has come to me !"
And she fain would go, as she whispers low—
" Mentone, I am waiting on thee !"
So they sailed away,
In the moonlight gray,
From the lady's balconie.

1870.

IN MATRIS MEMORIAM.

[Obiit 23rd January, 1871.]

OFT have we seen within some cottage small
    Black-bordered card, or sheet, in humble frame ;
Some " IN MEMORIAM " hung upon the wall,
    " *In memory of* "—what now is but a name !

I, who have tried before some truths to weave
    In humble verse—in very simplest song,
Now sing of one whose loss we sadly grieve—
    Whose memory dear our hearts will cherish long.

O dear departed MOTHER ! 'tis thy death
    That fills our hearts with grief too deep for tears :
We mourn thee now ; and, till our latest breath,
    Sweet thoughts of thee will fill the future years.

Up in my heart come memories of the past,
    In which thy cherished form most sadly blends ;
Thou who hast gone from out our life at last,
    The dearest, kindest, best of earthly friends !

I need not try to write her virtues here,
  So dear she was,—so loving, kind, and true ;
Let friends who knew her drop the tribute tear,—
  A wife's and mother's love *we only* knew.

Around we see dear traces of her hand ;
  . These tender touches tell the love she bore :
But she has gone into the Silent Land,
  And we must mourn her here for evermore.

Though still to us no silent land is this :
  For God is GOD ; there is a HEAVEN on high ;
And she is there, in that far land of bliss,
  Beyond the sun, above the azure sky.

No sickness, pain, no darkness, tears, nor care,
  But joyous song doth blend with cherub's tone ;
THOU whom the angels praise, hear now our prayer :
  Help us to find our lost one at Thy throne !

1871.

ABSENT FRIENDS.

HAST thou wandered in the woodland
    In the falling of the year,
When the leaves came fluttering downward,
    Dead and yellow, dry and sere?
Hast thou missed the friends who left thee,
    Weary-hearted and alone?
Hast thou missed the *form* beside thee,
    And the arm within thy own?

Hast thou sat around the table
    When the festive board was crowned,
When our hearts were filled with loving,
    As the laughter circled round?
Hast thou heard through all the talking,
    Hast thou heard through all the noise,
Some sweet *voice* upon thee calling—
    One who shared not in thy joys?

Hast thou mused within the shadow
  When the lamp was burning low?
Hast thou seen some dear *face* flicker
  In the firelight's ruddy glow?
Hath a loving and a longing
  (For a love with longing blends)
Ever filled thy weary spirit
  In the absence of thy friends?

1871.

WAE'S ME!

I LO'ED him weel,
I lo'ed him weel;
His form was fair;
His curly hair
Was black's the slae,
Noo mine is gray;
But still maun I,
Wi' sab an' sigh,
Wi' grief an' woe,
Think o' a joe,
Sae fair to see—
Wae's me! wae's me!

I lo'ed him weel,
I lo'ed him weel,
His heart was leal,
He askit me
If I wad be
Guidwife to him :

My een were dim,
My heart was fou,
I promised true ;
I wasna loth
To plight my troth ;
There's nane could be
Sae true as he—
Wae's me ! wae's me !

I lo'ed him weel,
I lo'ed him weel,
Puir Wully Steele !
Our names were cried,
Our hearts were tied,
We'd fain be ane ;
But HIM abune
Had grief decreed,—
My laddie dee'd
Before the day
Could join the twae.
A bride, ye see,
I still maun be—
Wae's me ! wae's me !

·1871.

THE MAID OF NORWAY:

A Ballad.

[*Queen Margaret, "the Maid of Norway," was daughter of the King of Norway, and grand-daughter of Alexander III. of Scotland. She died* 1290 A.D.]

THE King is dead in Auld Scotland,
 And never a son has he;
For they are dead, and he is dead,
 Dool comes fu' pitifullie.

The knights they lookit at the crown
 And wondered whase 'twad be;
Sir Michael * said,—" There is Margaret
 In Norroway over the sea."

" Woe to the land whose ruler's a child,"—
 The lang-faced priest doth say;
" But she maun hae her ain, she maun sit on the
  throne,
 Betide us it weel or wae."

---

  * Sir Michael Scott, of Balwearie.

So they got them a ship, and they sailed away,
    Away to a distant land,
To fetch them a Queen they had not seen
    To rule in Auld Scotland.

The gude knights hied them to Norroway
    For the maiden sae fair to see ;
And they bore her gently into the gude ship,
    And treated her tenderlie.

Sir Michael, the wizard weird and auld,
    Wi' beard like drifted snaw,
He watched the night when the moon was bright,
    To see where the wind did blaw.

Sir Michael he looked at the stars,
    And then he made his grane ;
For the King was dead, and his sons were dead,
    And this maiden was left alane.

This maiden fair he loved sae weel,
    As he watched her sport and play
At the good ship's side, as they crossed the tide
    From the land of Norroway.

But a cauld wind blew from the north ;
  Black grew baith sky and sea ;
And the little maid, sweet Margaret,
  She laid her down to dee.

As flower that's nippit in the bud
  When the north comes cauld and wild,
The wind blew ere the good knights knew,
  And killed the bonnie child.

They stood ilk yin around her bed,
  And watched the bairnie fair ;
Wi' tender grace they kissed her face,
  And stroked her gowden hair.

Sir Michael, he streakit her out,
  As still and pale she lay ;
The King, and his sons, and the maid were dead,
  And his heart was fou o' wae.

1871.

GOOD NIGHT!

THE darkness now is falling,
　　The parlour gas is lit;
And nursie's on me calling
　　To go to bed: 'Tis fit.
And Mamma dear will kiss me,
　　Her little cherub bright;
Though dear Papa should miss me,
　　I still must say, Good night!
　　　Good night, Mamma, Good night!

The birds have ceased their winging,
　　The sun now hides his head;
When birdies are not singing,
　　'Tis time for me to bed.
I'll hide me snug and cosie
　　Till comes the morning light;
Till gleams the sunlight rosy,
　　I'll bid you both, Good night!
　　　Papa, Mamma, Good night!

1871.

HER WAY O' HER AIN.

Is'T why dae I loe ye? my dearie!
   Is't hoo dae I loe sae weel?
Oh! I'm half vexed I ever cam' near ye;
   Ye dinna ken right hoo I feel.
What gars ye sic questions be speirin'?
   Tae answer I'm no very fain;
Come near and I'll tell in yer hearin'—
   I like that bit way o' yer ain—
   That laughin' wee way o' yer ain.

Ye ken that the rose o' the simmer
   Is red when it blooms on the tree;
I ken that your cheek gars't look dimmer
   Than ever I thought it to be.
But it's no that ye're bonnie, my lassie,
   Tho' a fairer I ken there is nane;
I loe ye where nane can surpass ye,
   For that darlin' wee way o' yer ain—
   That canty bit way o' yer ain.

N

Yon lily sae snaw-white an' slender
   Is bonny an' gracefu' an' tall ;
But you are more lovely an' tender,
   An' fairer an' sweeter than all.
The glint o' yer blue e'e is bonny,
   E'en that my heart's love couldna' gain ;
But o' lasses wha ever saw ony
   That had sic a way o' their ain—
   Sic a canny sweet way o' their ain ?

Noo, Leezie ! my coorin' wee dooie,
   Here, listen ! let naebody ken,
Sae weel, my dear lass, do I loe ye,
   I've ta'en a bit but an' a ben.
Will ye share my wee biggin', my Leezie ?
   I'm tired noo wi' livin' my lane ;
I ken ye'll say " Ay," just to please me,
   Ye've got sic a way o' yer ain—
   Sic a charmin' wee way o' yer ain.

1871.

THE OLD PIANO.

Up-stairs in a room which is never used,
 The old piano stands;
Its case is good, but the strings are loosed,
 And the music which loving hands
Could draw from its keys, so yellow and old,
 ·Has vanished for ever and fled;—
A music whose sweetness can never be told
 Has passed with the years which are dead.

Still a vision of jewelled hands I see
 Flit over its ivory notes,—
Sweet snow-white hands which were dear to me:
 And a liquid melody floats
Through the darkened room where I stand alone;
 The echoes for ever remain
Of the songs *she* sang in such a tone,
 And the music is still in my brain.

Ah ! many a year has passed away ;
   Still the old piano stands
In a room which is veiled from the light of day :
   No longer her gentle hands
Touch these sweet strings ; but a richer chord
   She strikes on her harp, I deem,
In a sweet voice praising her blessed Lord,
   In the midst of the cherubim.

1871.

GOOD-BYE.

ALONG the lane, beneath the trees,
  They wandered in the dawning gray;
Poor meek-eyed Jessie, weeping, sees
  Her love a little on his way.
Down to the turn where grows the thorn,
  She pauses there, with sob and sigh;
Her gentle breast with grief is torn,
  As there she bids her love Good-bye.

Weeks grow to months, and months to years;
  The town is full of maids and men;
And Jessie whispers through her tears,
  When wandering down the lonely glen,—
"Some other love has stolen from me
  My dearest love, and I will die!—
Farewell! farewell! Ah! can it be
  Yon parting was our last Good-bye?"

Weeks grow to months, and months to years;
  Full oft has bloomed the hawthorn tree;
Confirmed she thought were all her fears,
  Her love she never more would see.
One eve, as gentle gloaming fell,
  She met him with a happy cry;
As up the lane he came to tell,—
  " Yon parting *was* our last Good-bye !"

1873.

STEER STRAIGHT FOR ME!

SKIPPING and tripping,
    With laughter light,
The boys went scampering down to the shore :
Merrily, happily, plying the oar,
    They sail away, for the sun is bright.
        In capital time
        They gently dip
Their oars in a glittering sea of gold,
And they make for the isle with the castle old,
    There to waken the echoes with laughing lip.

        Suddenly ceased they
        Their childish joys,
When a mist came rolling up out of the west
(For children are children, you know, at the best),
    And I set out to bring over my boys.
        The night it grew dark,
        And I could not see,
And I missed my way in the blinding rain,
Till a childish cry came over the main,—
    " O Father ! my Father ! steer straight for me ! "

    'Twas Jamie that cried, sir,
    From over the sea :
The poor little fellow is dead many years,
But cheerfully still rings the voice in my ears ;
  And it sounds more sweet than it used to be
     In the silent night
     So soft and low,—
" *Steer straight for me !* " Is there mist from the west ?—
Comes the voice from the Heaven where he is at rest,
  When around me are clouds, and the hurricanes blow.

   1874.

AT *SOMEWHERE* HALL.

THERE, beneath ivy and rose,
    Over a door that I love,
Seen when the wind gently blows,
    Stirring the roses above,
A curious thing has been hid
    By credulous people of old—
A horse-shoe the ivy amid,
    Put there for luck, I am told.

Wonderful things it has seen,
    Hidden up there 'neath the rose;
How many passers have been
    Under it nobody knows.
Some foot the threshold has passed,
    To cross it again never more :
Some have been carried at last
    Awkwardly out at the door.

Partings and welcomings, too,
    Now and then laughter and tears ;
Under the rusty horse-shoe,
    Much has been seen in the years.
Lovers ! ah, well—one I know,
    She won't the secret unfold ;
Just here where the roses blow,
    Have been partings that cannot be told.

In luck there is no one believes :
    Would it be wicked to say
To the thing under the leaves,—
    " Keep every evil away ?
Guard, as you have done before,
    A maiden exceedingly fair ;
Keep ever out at the door
    Disaster and sorrow and care !"

LOVED AND LOST.

O LOVED AND LOST!   O loved and lost!
   That words were weak I never knew,
Till when thy path my footsteps crossed
   I tried to tell my love to you.

O breaking heart! O throbbing brow!
   That words are few it may be well,
For surely no one knew till now
   A love—a loss—no one can tell:

A love which in my bosom burned,
   And grateful filled my heart and soul!
Blindly to thee my being turned,
   As turns the needle to the pole.

O good and true! no fault was thine
   That for my love you did not care;
If blame there be 'tis only mine:
   'Twas God that made thee good and fair.

My love was earnest, true, and deep,
　And lasted long before I told;
But when the secret would not keep,
　I whispered soft the story old.

O happy time ! O golden years !
　O dream ! what pain thy wakening cost;
An answer came through blinding tears—
　I found that I had loved and lost !

1874.

OUR TWIN BOYS.

[These were the Author's nephews.   They died 3rd October,
1874, aged six days.]

Joy and sorrow, grief and gladness
  Mingle in this life of ours ;
Now our hearts are filled with sadness ;—
  Oh ! the weary, weary hours !
We have sorrows more than joys,
For we mourn our infant boys,
And our eyes are dim with tears,
  And our hearts are sad and lonely,
  That they visited us only,—
Did not stay throughout the years.

Smooth the fingers gently, sweetly,
  Wrap the little limbs in white ;
Kiss the eyelids down completely ;
  Bid the babes a last "Good night !"
Though our eyes are dim with tears,
Rises hope above our fears,

And our hearts should joyous be
   That our babies they will never
   Know of sorrow now or ever :
They are happier than we.

Far away we gaze intently ;
   They are now where nothing harms,
Folded carefully and gently
   In the EVERLASTING ARMS.
Let our hearts, then, beat with love
For our infant sons above ;
We nor murmur nor complain.
   Said the CHRIST of Galilee—
   "Let the children come to Me."
Has He asked from us in vain ?

1874.

I LOVE MY LOVE.

"I LOVE my love !"—the theme is old,
  A thousand times it has been sung ;
The story has been often told
  By youth and maid since time was young.
'Tis ever old—'tis ever new,
  Yet care not I how old it be,
For every day doth prove it true—
  "I love my love, and he loves me !"

Eight little words, in one sweet row,
  Contain much more, you must agree,
Than many volumes that you know :—
  "I love my love, and he loves me."
Of history, fable, tale, and song
  The burden this doth still remain ;
Of letter, legend, story long,
  "I love my love "—is the refrain.

I say it when the night is still ;
 To my own heart I whisper low,
When silence broods on vale and hill,
 These dear old words of long ago.
" I love my love—I love my love."—
 What music sweet as this can be ?
A truth all other truths above—
 " I love my love ; he loveth me !"

1875.

UNBAPTISED:

A NORTHAMPTONSHIRE IDYLL.

THE woman did wait on the haughty priest ;
 With a broken voice—" O sir ! " she said,
 " I only want to bury my dead."
He did not speak till the sobbing ceased ;
The weeping and wailing he did not heed ;
Callous and cold, with his pitiless creed,
What does he care for the eyes tear-wet ?
  No pity has he :—
  " Oh, it cannot be,
But in unblest ground when the sun is set."

The night-owl hoots in the old church-tower—
 Hear ye the wail of the wintry breeze
 Through the naked arms of the creaking trees ?
The night is as dark as at midnight hour ;
The sexton is busy with mattock and spade—
Ere the hour is struck must the grave be made.
The watch-dog howls to the starless sky :
  Cast the spade in the mould,
  Now the hour is tolled,
And the earth will be shovelled in by and by.

Five maidens they carry a coffin there—
    Slowly they move o'er the village green,
    And flickering lanterns glimmer between.
The mourners are bearing their burden with care ;
Heart-broken they pass through the churchyard gate;
At unhallowed grave doth the sexton wait :
Hurriedly will he his work complete.
        " Hell Corner " is this—
        What business is his ?
The vicar has told him the place is most meet.

The coffin just lowered contains but a child,
    Pure as the snow, or its winding sheet.
    From the thorny ways of the world its feet
Have been taken away, and ONE more mild
Than the heartless priest has never despised
The cast-out infant—the unbaptised :
" *Suffer the children to come unto Me !* "
        Does the priest not know
        That, long ago,
It was said that of such must the Kingdom be ?

1876.

A FRAGMENT FROM GOETHE'S LIFE.

Dramatis Personæ—GOETHE, AMELIA, LUCINDA.

Scene—The Parlour of a House in Strasbourg. Enter
GOETHE.

GOETHE.

Amelia, my love! my dearest!
Are you ill?

AMELIA.

Hush, Goethe! gently! No, I am not ill,
Neither am I your dearest, nor your love;
But one who would be both—Lucinda—
She is ill. You take my hand! be seated here,
For I have much to say; you must be still,
And listen only while I speak.

GOETHE.

What of Lucinda—is she very ill?

AMELIA.

You were to listen only while *I* spoke ;
Speak not at all, unless you speak so low
No ears but mine may hear.   Lucinda sleeps ;
Her bedroom is above.

GOETHE.

I will not speak at all ; 'tis sweet enough
To listen to your voice—even when you chide ;
And when you whisper low, as now you do,
Sweet music thrills me—beating on my brain.

AMELIA.

'Tis of Lucinda that I fain would speak ;
Yes, she is ill, dear Goethe—very ill.
You read to us of that sweet English maid
Who sickened for her love, and never told :
My sister has her plaint—you know it well ;
I think she'll surely die, she loves you so !

GOETHE.

I never gave her cause.

AMELIA.

You made no love to her, yet cause enough
She had to love you well.   What woman can

Resist your charms, dear Goethe ?   Had not I
Loved well my love—my sweetheart far away,
Before you crossed the threshold of our door,
I might have been as she, and even now
Fearing, I tremble for my plighted troth.

GOETHE.

Be mine, then ! mine ! my darling, come with me !
How often have I said, I love you well !
Far better than——

AMELIA.

Oh ! hush ! hush !—there, be still ! it cannot be !
I love my love—to him I will be true;
And to be true, and for Lucinda's sake,
This day, for ever, must we say—farewell !
Ay, even now, dear Goethe, you must go.
How hard it is for me, I cannot tell ;
And she—my sister—surely she will die
Heart-broken.

GOETHE.

What ! in tears, Amelia ?   Well, I will go.
Perhaps 'tis better that I should.

AMELIA.

Yes, yes; it must be so! I lead you out.
O Goethe, Goethe!—fare-thee-well—farewell!
For ever, Goethe! I do love my love,
But yet for once——

                [Embracing him.

(Lucinda rushes in, in dishabille.)

LUCINDA.

Not only you! not only you!
Yes, I.am mad! I also will for once
Take Goethe in my arms.

                [Embracing him.

Farewell—farewell! Thy head between my hands,
Dear Goethe, with my cheek thus close to thine,
My dark hair laid against thy golden curls,
My arm about thy neck—for once, just once—
One kiss!—the first and last—farewell! farewell!
Goethe, I bless thee!—*but my curse on her*
Who first shall touch these sweet lips after me—
Woe, woe, unutterable!—darkness and despair!
Sister, stand back! Goethe, begone!—begone!

1874.

Humorous Poems.

"SPEIRING THE GUIDWULL."

THE moon was shinin' bricht an' fair,
    The wind blew cauld across the muir,
As Robbie Bell, spried-up an' clean,
Wi' weel-spun hose an' buckled shoon,
In shepherd's plaid, an' bannet blue,
Gaed yont tae see "his cushie doo,"
A weel-faur'd lass, a sonsie queen—
Faith ! he was prood o' bonny Jean.

At kirk or market sly was she,
Took unco care that nane wad see
The look she meant for Rab himsel';
In troth, the neebours couldna tell
Whether she liked the lad or no—
The mair she'd like, the less she'd show;
But weel kent Rab, an' him alane,
That a' her heart was a' his ain.

Doon by the wimplin' burnie's side,
Where droopin' birks an' willows hide
Fond lovers frae a' pryin' een,
Rab aft had courted bonny Jean—
Had sweetly preed her cherry mou',
Had ca'd her een sweet, saft, an' blue,
Had fum'led wi' her gowden hair,
An' praised her charms in Doric rare.

But tho' Rab courted geyan slee,
Fair Jeanie's mither fine could see
Hoo lay the land, an' unco weel
Was pleased that sic a wiselike chiel
Should efter Jean.   Did she no ken
That Rab had ta'en a but an' ben?—
Full prood the wifie was tae learn
O' guid doon-sittin' for her bairn.

Wi' anxious heart, across the hill
Rab gaed a-speirin' the guidwull.
When Jeanie heard his whustle clear,
She slippit out; she wadna hear
The story he had come to tell.
Auld Tammas likit Robbie Bell,
An' weel she wot he's sure to tak'
The offer Robbie comes to mak'.

The tale's sune telled : Auld Tam agrees,
An' Jeanie's mither, laughin', sees
Rab lookin' for his darlin' lass.
But, bide a wee, he still maun pass
Another trial :—" The but an' ben,
A canty biggin' doon the glen,
Is fine," says Tam ;—" but has he poo'r
O' utterance when comes the 'oor ? "

The " big ha' Bible " frae its place,
Tam hands tae Rab, looks in his face,
An' layin't on the laddie's knees,
Says,—" Rab, *ye'll tak' the exerceese.*"
Wi' reverent look, the bannet blue
Is doffed ; he reads the chapter through :
In trembling voice he tries to pray ;—
Ootside fair Jeanie's listenin' tae.

Noo a' is dune, an' by the han'
Tam grippin' Rab, says,—" Ye're the man ;"
An' Jeanie's mither gangs tae see
" Whar can that glaikit lassie be ; "
But Jeanie, wi' her heart at mou',
Comes in tae see her laddie noo ;
An' Rab gangs whustlin' ower the hill,
Weel satisfied he's " speired their wull."

O Scotland dear ! I love thee well :
Dear to my heart is hill and dell,
Dear, rocky glen, and ferny scaur,
Dear, mountain peak ; but dearer far
These annals of a bygone time,
Howe'er uncouthly shaped in rhyme.
'Tis well the poet sweetly sings—
" From scenes like these our grandeur springs."

1870.

LUCIFER LOWE.

[*In reference to the Tax upon Lucifer Matches proposed
in the Budget, April,* 1871.]

MR. LUCIFER LOWE has proposed
    A tax the other night ;
When the Budget is fully disclosed,
    The tax it won't be *light*.

Financial Bob, you may know—
    A *matchless* Bob is he—
Finds the funds are rather *low ;*
    Now this should never be.

" A curious smile he smole,
    A knowing wink he wunk ;"
More money's of course his goal,
    And he has plenty *spunk*.

" O Lucifer ! how art thou fallen ! "
    'Tis thus it once was phrased ;
But now will the boys be calling—
    The lucifers all are raised.

On the Sun there once was a tax
   (Our window-frames, you know) :
To the lights which strike on the box
   Is descending rather *low*.

Vesuvians, tapers, fusees !
   Well, this is a ha'penny catch ;
And I'm sure the country sees
   The Chancellor hasn't a *match*.

Take care, Mr. Lucifer Lowe,
   In case you extinguished be !
Such taxes, they won't do now,
   In the light of this century.

1871.

SANDY HEW AT SEA.

[AFTER HOOD.]

AH ! Sandy won't forget the day
   Remembered well by me ;
Not much he'd *seen ;*—one winter morn
   He started off to *sea.*

The wind it blew a furious blast—
   A hurricane in fine ;
And Sandy swore a dreadful oath—
   To *blackball* was not his *line.*

A wink of sleep he never got,
   When tossing on his bunk ;
His eyes with terror stared full wide,
   His head was on a *trunk.*

He tossed and turned, and turned and tossed,
   Nor heard the sailors shout ;
Then still he lay : strange malady !—
   His *inside* wanted *out.*

The sea it poured upon the deck,
　The wind more fiercely blew ;
The sky was black, but Sandy was—
　Ah ! quite another *hue.*

His neighbour thought they would be wrecked :
　" I *see* a ship ! "—cried he ;
Alack ! alack ! it was not so ;
　They only *shipped* a *sea !*

But Sandy's philosophical
　Indifference was fine ;
He faintly wished he might be *cured*
　By being thrown in brine.

The ship which Lloyd had entered "*A,*"
　Was broken with the *sea ;*
And many wondered how it was
　That such a thing could *be.*

The water rushed into the hold,
　Each man he seized a pail ;
One Sandy shook, and called on him
　To come and *stand to bale.*　　·

It was in vain ; he heeded not ;
  One glance around he gave :
His eyes were very *watery*,
  His face was very *grave*.

Then Sandy he a lesson learned ;
  For many times he swore
He'd *see* the world : but now he vowed
  He'd never *sea* it more.

1871.

WINDYGOWL.

Wi' weary steps I lost my gait;
　.The nicht was dark as dark could be,
As up the glen I wandered late,
　　An' stumbled ower the grassy lea;
　　　　Nae siller mune
　　　　Cam', late or sune,
　　To guide the weary feet o' me.

Till through the mirk there gleamed a spark;
　　A gentle, feeble, flickerin' lowe
Cam' glintin' doonward through the dark,
　　Frae cottage window up the knowe—
　　　　A welcome sicht,
　　　　On sic a nicht,
　　To weary wanderer i' the howe.

The hearty laird o' Windygowl
　　Was sittin' porin' ower his book;
His watchfu' collie gied a growl,
　　He opes the door wi' cautious look—

" Ye've lost yer gate ?
Ye're unco late ;
Come in, man, to the ingle nook."

A broad bricht fire o' scented peat
    Threw lengthened shadows at oor back,
The collie curled up at oor feet,
    The dishes glittered in the rack,
        As cheek by jowl,
        At Windygowl,
    The laird an' me fell on the crack.

Said I,—" Guidman, what for d'ye ca'
    Yer place by sic a name sae queer ?
I've been in mony a hut an' ha'
    Less beild than this, baith far an' near."
        " Jist bide a wee,"—
        Quoth he to me,
    " Jist bide a wee ; ye're sure to hear."

A sough cam' roun' the auld hoose en',
    A weary, dreary sab an' sigh ;
It garr'd me grue, I didna ken ;
    'Twas like as if a ghost were by,
        Or bairnie wheengin',
        Greetin', peengin'—
    An eerie, eldrich, waesome cry.

P

A' roond the house, out-ower the byre,
    A ticht wind whistled clear an' free ;
Aneth the door it fanned the fire,
    The collie watched wi' blinkin' e'e ;
        It sabbed an' swirled,
        Grew laigh, then skirled :
The laird aye keep't his e'e on me.

It rantit, tantit, tore, an' swore,
    An' scrieched an' scrauched, a fearsome howl ;
It dashed an' slammed, cuist wide the door,
    Gaed up the lum wi' awfu' growl.
        The laird he chaffed,
        An' hotched an' laughed :—
"It's no ill-named, is't,—Windygowl ?"

'Tis mony a year noo sin' the day
    Aft up the glen I liked to ca' ;
The roof's been lang since blawn away
    An' Windygowl's but broken wa' ;
        The guid auld laird 's
        In the kirkyaird,
An' winter winds still wail an' blaw.

1875.

THE MISOGAMIST.

"I HATE the women; 'tis no cant,—
　A vain, conceited, frivolous crew;
They're only fit to dress and flaunt
　In feathers, ribbons, red and blue,—
In frill and flounce, with lace and veil;
　They love the pretty, not the true;
They're facile, fickle, feeble, frail—
　Why need I further swell the list?
Their foolishness is nothing new:"—
　Remarked this strange Misogamist.

"They chatter, clatter, never cease
　To gossip scandal at their tea;
They whisper mischief, break the peace,
　And kiss, and hate, and disagree,
With sob and sigh, or smile and tear,
　The hollowness of which you see;"
Then summing up with bitter sneer,—
　"Their life's a trifle; they insist
On chronicling the smallest beer:"—
　So said this wild Misogamist.

I did not like his spiteful talk ;
　　I did not see him for a year :
One winter night, in homeward walk,
　　I heard a voice,—" Cling closer, dear."
Although 'twas long since last we met,
　　I knew the tones ; 'twas very queer ;
A husband now without regret :
　　Two ruddy lips as ere were kissed,
Remarked full low,—" I thank you, pet,"
　　To this same mad. Misogamist.

1875.

THE AULD KIRK BELL OF DALKEITH.

O YE wha in the city dwells,
I envy ye yer walth o' bells :
Frae steeple, turret, belfry, toor,
They tinkle music every 'oor.
A hundred hammers rise an' fa',
A hundred bells, baith big an sma',
    Deep-toned an' low,
Their music mingle, yin an' a'
     Wi' measure slow.

Or ye wha in some lowland glen,
Far frae the noisy haunts o' men,
When sunlight glints upon the corn,
Hear, on the silent Sabbath morn,
The bell which beats the call to prayer
Come ringing in the morning air,
    Sae clear an' sweet,
As to God's house the folk repair
     Wi' sober feet.

'Tis sweet to hear the soonds o' bells
That rise an' fa' wi' sobs an' swells;
That ring, an' peal, an' beat, an' chime,
An' strike the music oot wi' time.
But waesome is the soond o' oors,
It dunts an' dunners, clanks an' cloors—
    An awfu' din;
It bangs an' smashes oot the 'oors,
    Baith late an' sune.

Oft hae we heard it said an' sung—
The memory o' bells which rung
In childhood's days are dear to them
In foreign lands wha mak' their hame;
But nae sic recollections dear
Will fash the bairnies noo wha here-
    Aboot do.dwell:
A melancholy clankin' drear
    Mak's oor kirk bell.

1876.

THE GALLOWAY WIFE.

[*An old Ballad giving an account of the origin of an old family,
the Sprots of Urr.*]

YE'LL a' hae heard tell o' the Galloway wife,
    A wonderfu' woman was she;
An' hoo she endit the bloody strife
    'Tween the King an' the Sotherns three.

At first they were fechtin' three to yin,
    An' syne there was only twa,
An' syne there was only yin to yin,
    But she didna ken wha was wha.

At last she heard the Sothern's aith,
    An' then she grippit his hair,
An' poo'd them doon and stoppit them baith,
    An' the King stood laughin' there.

" An' wha are ye, my canty wife ? "—
    The guid King Robert speired,
" That daured to meddle in this strife :
    Guidsakes ! ye wasna feared.

" An' whar's yer hoose ? is't far awa ?
  (Rise, Selby, there's my hand)
I haena tasted meat the day,
  An' this my ain Scotland."

" My hoose is here, across the burn,
  Richt welcome will ye be ;
But weel I wot this English knight
  Will get nae meat frae me."

They sat them doon by her fireside,
  She poored the scaldin' broo,
An' a' her spoons she weel did hide,
  But the yin the King should hae.

" An' noo, guidwife, till I be dune
  I'll gar ye earn yer fee,
An' a' the land ye can rin roond
  I'll gie in gift to thee."

She rowed her sleeves, her hair she bund,
  She kilted to the knee,
Adoon the brae, afore the wind,
  She flew to earn her fee.

Adoon the brae, an' through the glen,
  She jumpit ower the burn ;
A wily fox had stown her hen,—
  Her head she wadna turn.

The miller's asleep on his sheilin' knowe,
  The mill itsel' was on fire ;
" Aweel,"—says she,—" jist let it lowe,"
  As she jumpit ower bush an' brier.

Four horses are lowse by the burnie's side,
  Wi' saddles an' bridles fine,
For a helmet o' gold she wadna bide :
  " I will get them a' when I'm dune.

" I weel I wot I've run fu' fast,
  But the King will be dune,"—said she,
An' back she flew to her hoose at last,
  An' keekit in to see.

The King an' Sir Selby sat side-by-side,
  The brose it was nearly dune,
An' there wi' the yin that she didna hide
  It was time aboot wi' the spoon.

Q

An' this is the tale o' the Galloway wife,
   An' a wonderfu' wife was she ;
An' a' the land that she did rin roond
   The King as a gift did gie.

1877.

THE END.

2 8 7 0 7 4

LORIMER AND GILLIES, PRINTERS, 31 ST. ANDREW SQUARE, EDINBURGH.

www.ingramcontent.com/pod-product-compliance
Lightning Source LLC
Chambersburg PA
CBHW030645030726
47497CB00006B/1955